THE MIRROR'S SECRET

BY KATHY FRONHEISER

D0834998

The Mirror's Secret
Copyright © 2019 by Kathy Fronheiser

Published by
Far Off Lands Publishing
Denver, Colorado

All rights reserved.

No part of this book may be reproduced in any form or by any electronic or mechanical means, including information storage and retrieval systems, without written permission from the author, except in the case of a reviewer, who may quote brief passages embodied in critical articles or in a review.

This is a work of fiction. Names, characters, places, and incidents either are the product of the author's imagination or are used fictitiously, and any resemblance to actual persons, living or dead, events, or locales is entirely coincidental.

Book cover design by bravoboy.
Interior book design by YellowStudios.

ISBN: 978-1-7330364-0-5
Library of Congress Control Number: 2019908223

Printed in the United States of America

For my daughter, Bonnie

"Time is the longest distance between two places."

—Tennessee Williams

PROLOGUE

Hanover, Pennsylvania
June 30, 1863

D r. Grant Alexander bent over a bleeding Union soldier sprawled on top of the grand piano in the parlor, surrounded by countless other wounded men. Another artillery shell exploded nearby, shaking the walls of the large stone house that had overnight become his hospital. The bloodied knife slipped from his hand and clattered across the wood floor.

An inhuman cry emerged from the lips of the dying man before him. Grant wrapped the soldier's trembling hand in his own and spoke to him in soft, soothing tones as if they were the only two people in the room. Gentle reassurance would do him more good than surgery at this point. The chloroform was running short anyway. He watched the man's face as he whispered to him of courage, good deeds done, home and loved ones. Soon peace and calm blanketed the anguish of his pain. Another lost soul.

Just as Grant called out through the chaos to his assistant, a deafening explosion shook the walls. He raised his eyes in time to see the room above crash through the ceiling, burying him in the rubble with the dead soldier still clutching his hand.

llie Michaels inserted her key into the front door deadbolt of Ivy Garden Inn as she had so many times since her aunt bought the property three years ago. Pushing the heavy oak door aside, she stepped into the front parlor and dropped her bags on the carpet.

Out of the corner of her eye, she caught a wisp of white flickering in the antique mirror. She walked toward it to touch the surface where she'd seen the white shadow but was stopped by a wall of cold air. Shivering, she buttoned her cardigan sweater and rubbed her arms. A few steps backward and the temperature of the room returned to normal. A cold spot, she thought as she wiped away a tear. A small area of concentrated psychic energy was all that remained of the dear woman who had raised her and put her through nursing school. The cold seemed to seep into her bones, along with a weird sense of soft electrical current. It had to be her.

"I'm sorry, Aunt Carolyn. I'm so sorry." Ellie spoke to the empty room, turning around in a circle to make sure she'd addressed every corner. Her voice echoed in the stillness. If her words couldn't reach Aunt Carolyn's spirit, then she'd apologize to her furnishings, the lovely antiques they'd picked out together on the weekends when Ellie visited. She knew how much Aunt Carolyn needed her and yet she stayed in New York. All the promises she'd made ran through her mind in mocking whispers. "I can't quit my job at the hospital just yet, Aunt Carolyn, but I'll come in the spring when things aren't quite so hectic. Then I'll move in and help you." How empty and senseless those reasons seemed to her now. It was too late. Again, a flicker of white made her turn toward the mirror, but it vanished as soon as she faced it.

"Get a grip on yourself," she muttered as she blew her nose and dried her tears. Carrying her bags into the small modern apartment at the back of the inn, she inhaled faint aroma of vanilla that still hung in the air, the scent of Aunt Carolyn's favorite skin lotion. The comforting smell Ellie remembered from her childhood hadn't changed over the years. She closed her eyes and took in the fading scent, vowing to cling to every shred of her aunt's presence for as long as she could.

In accordance with Aunt Carolyn's wishes, there would be a short afternoon funeral service followed by the burial in the town cemetery. Carolyn Louise Michaels would fade from the earth as the late afternoon sun faded from the sky. As hard as she had tried to prepare the eulogy, Ellie still wasn't exactly sure what she would say when she heard the minister announce, "And now, Carolyn's dear niece, Ellen, would like to say a few words."

Maybe after speaking to the townspeople, the employees from the inn and others she expected to come by to pay their respects, her thoughts would come together. She sure hoped there'd be no surprises in the coming days. It hadn't occurred to her until now that some distant relative might appear, someone she'd never even heard of. Shirttail relations had a way of surfacing at times like this, especially when an inheritance was involved. Well, she'd handle whatever situation arose once the service was over. The last thing she wanted was for Aunt Carolyn to be disappointed in her sendoff. Ellie knew her aunt better than anyone in the world and would do everything possible to honor her memory at the church service the following afternoon.

Before sitting down with her tablet to prepare some notes, she checked Aunt Carolyn's pantry for something to eat and found it filled with choices. Aunt Carolyn was probably preparing something for her guests when her heart gave out. By the time the housekeeper found her collapsed on the kitchen floor, it was too late to save her. Not such a bad way to go, really. Better than lingering in pain and misery the way she'd seen so many do in her years as a nurse. Still, death dealt a terrible blow to those left behind when it happened this way.

Ellie kept expecting to see her aunt come around the corner into the kitchen, humming to herself the way she always did.

Although she'd had no appetite when she left New York early that morning, it seemed a good idea to fortify herself for the afternoon ahead. By the time she'd finished a bowl of soup, the page and a half of notes on the tablet she scribbled on eased her concerns about speaking at the service.

Ellie carried her robe and toiletries into the bathroom and took a long hot shower. She piled her long curls on top of her head and massaged citrus shampoo into her scalp. Then she scrubbed her skin and washed her hair again. Although she knew it was impossible to scour away remorse, she gave it a good try.

On the afternoon of the funeral, Ellie was glad she didn't have to make any decisions about what to wear. She only owned one black dress, which she kept for rare occasions like this. The dark silk felt foreign to her, so different from the brightly colored prints she usually wore. She slipped her tiny feet into a pair of black pumps that still looked brand new.

Ellie glanced at her watch. Better move faster. Where had she put her pearls? They must be here somewhere. She remembered unpacking the jewelry case. Those pearls had once belonged to her mother. So beautiful and so precious. How could she have lost them? It was important to Ellie that some part of her mother be there today to bid farewell to Aunt Carolyn. She had to find them.

On the verge of tears once again, she went through everything in her bag in a panic, hurling each item over her shoulder after reassuring herself the pearls weren't embedded in it.

She even went outside to the car. Her SUV had plenty of room in the back. Maybe somehow the pearls slid out of her bag, but a thorough search revealed nothing. She slammed the car doors and hurried back inside.

Frozen in the doorway of the bedroom, she stared at the top of the dresser. Arranged in a neat circle on top of the jewelry case were her pearls. They hadn't been there a few minutes ago. She was positive of that. Easing herself down on the edge of the bed, she put her hands over her face and took a deep shaky breath, half expecting the pearls to be gone when she opened her eyes. To her relief, they were still there.

Deciding that Aunt Carolyn must have become her guardian angel, she glanced around the room and whispered a soft thank you before clasping the pearls around her neck and heading out the door, still shaking her head in amazement at what had just happened.

Aside from instructing Alice, the housekeeper, to take Aunt Carolyn's navy suit with white trim and some matching jewelry to the funeral director, Ellie couldn't recall making many decisions. As with so many other aspects of her life, Aunt Carolyn had carefully planned and fully paid for her funeral arrangements. Ellie had only been able to pull herself together enough to access the inn's website from home and cancel existing reservations for the next few weeks with apologies.

Arriving well before the start of the service, Ellie spent the time shaking countless hands, accepting condolences and seeing to the inevitable last-minute details. The short but dignified church service turned out to be exactly what Aunt Carolyn would have wanted, and Ellie was pleased at the number of people who attended and pleased that she found exactly the right words when her turn came to speak.

At the cemetery she hung back to linger a while after everyone had left, not ready to take that final step in the physical process of letting go. The emotional process would take a lot longer. She felt the weight of unspoken words adding to the heaviness in her heart. Goodbye and Thank You were at the top of the list, but they seemed so inadequate. The earlier sunshine was replaced with darkening clouds and strengthening wind, the skies reflecting her grief. Another tear spilled onto her cheek.

"Excuse me." A young man approached her with his hands in the pockets of his pants. He wore thick dark rimmed glasses with frames that matched his hair. A flat mixture of brown and black with no style. "Just wanted to say how sorry I am about your aunt. Fine woman."

"Do I know you?" Ellie asked, brushing away her tears. She remembered seeing him sitting alone in the back of the church during the service but hadn't recognized him.

"Probably not." He pulled his right hand out of his pocket and extended it, grasping hers in a tight sweaty grip and giving it a single shake downward before letting go. "Wade," he said. "Wade Savage."

"How do you know my aunt?"

"The inn," he replied, as if that explained everything.

"Have you been a guest at Ivy Garden?"

"No. Not exactly. Grew up here in Hanover and always loved that old stone house. I knew the previous owners quite well. Wanted to buy it when it went up for sale three years ago, but Miss Carolyn, may she rest in peace, outbid me."

"I see."

"Expect to sell it, now that she's gone?"

The question took Ellie by surprise. First this guy intrudes on her final moments with Aunt Carolyn, then he wants to make a deal right here in the cemetery. "Aunt Carolyn isn't even in the ground yet and already you want to move in and take her place?" How dare he?

Wade shuffled his feet and studied the toes of his shoes but didn't respond.

"This is hardly the time to discuss it," Ellie went on. "I can only tell you at this point that I haven't made any decisions."

"Understand." He worked at picking a piece of white lint off the front of his tweed blazer. After a long pause, he said, "Well, I'd like to come by." He flicked the bit of lint away and inspected the lapels to make sure there were no others. Then he raised his head to look at her while he finished his sentence. "To talk with you. Plan to be around long?"

"I'm really not sure. As I already told you, I haven't made any decisions." She turned away from him and took a step closer to Aunt Carolyn.

"All right then." He nodded, hunched his shoulders, and sauntered away.

Wade Savage's rude intrusion shattered the reverent atmosphere from the graveside service. She touched the casket one last time. "I love you, Aunt Carolyn," she whispered. "I'll never forget you." Turning the collar of her raincoat up to protect her neck from the wind, she walked back to her car, cold drizzle blending with the tears on her face.

Over the next few days, countless friends and acquaintances shook her hand, hugged her and did their best to comfort her. Aunt Carolyn certainly made an impression on the people she'd known here.

The weeks that followed blurred together in a tangle of errands, paperwork, tears of sadness, and smiles at fond memories. By the time the hospital where she'd been working approved her request for a leave of absence, Ellie knew she wasn't going back. How could she possibly leave the place she'd come to love so much? Sure, it would be different now with Aunt Carolyn gone but during the weeks that had passed since the funeral, Ivy Garden had started to feel like home.

She drove down to New York and was able to accomplish everything she needed to do in a single day. She got up early for the four-hour drive and stopped at the hospital first to turn in her resignation and sign papers to continue her health insurance. It was hard to say good-bye to all the people she'd worked with for so many years. Everyone wished her well in her new venture and many promised to come and visit Ivy Garden. Then, after all the apartment details were settled, she took one final walk through the neighborhood. Although this long chapter in her life was coming to an end, a new and exciting one was beginning. She had no regrets.

Now and then while going through Aunt Carolyn's things at the inn, she gave in to her grief and emotional exhaustion by allowing herself a day of much needed rest. At least she didn't have to worry about her lost income from her job at the hospital. Thankfully Aunt Carolyn had used her wise investments to purchase the inn so there were no mortgage payments to worry about. As long as Ellie made wise decisions going forward, her future was secure.

She had just finished the difficult task of boxing up the last of Aunt Carolyn's clothing for the local charity when the chime of the front doorbell made her jump.

Great. No makeup, grimy jeans and a sweatshirt with a hole in the sleeve. Heading toward the parlor, she pulled the elastic from her ponytail and shook her long hair loose, ruffling it with one hand as she walked. She stopped at the window long enough to draw the curtain aside just a little. Wade Savage stood on the front porch, fingering the stones alongside the doorframe.

"Oh. Yes. Hello," he said when she opened the door, as if she'd come to his house instead of the other way around.

"Wade Savage?"

"Yes. Ah, by the way, have you ever noticed this stonework on the front of the inn here, between the door and the corner of the porch?"

What was she supposed to say? "No. I hadn't noticed."

"It doesn't match. Hit by a Confederate shell and then repaired." He waited. "Anyway, can I come in?"

Ellie left the door open for him, then turned to watch him step inside without wiping his feet. "Please sit down," she said, then retraced her steps to close the door he'd left standing open, making a mental note to apply some spray-on carpet cleaner to erase his footprints after he left.

He stood in the middle of the room, examining the furnishings. "She's added a few more pieces since I was here last," he observed. "This wing chair here…"

"Was there something you wanted, or did you come here to take inventory of the furnishings?" She realized how nasty that sounded but didn't feel she owed him much courtesy after their encounter at the cemetery, even if he did know Aunt Carolyn. Ellie still couldn't recall her aunt ever mentioning him.

"Must apologize to you about that day at the cemetery. Didn't mean to intrude." He cleared his throat. "Should have been more considerate."

Okay. She'd give him the benefit of one more chance. "Let's put it behind us, shall we?" she suggested, "and start over?"

He appeared to be taking her offer under serious consideration. Generous of him.

She sat down in her favorite overstuffed chair and adjusted the doily on the arm while she waited for him to get around to the real purpose for his visit. Men like Wade didn't make a special trip to apologize in person for their own insensitivity. There had to be another reason.

"Yeah," he finally responded with a nod. "Great." He took a seat on the sofa. "If you don't mind, I'll sit here. I like the view of the room from this spot."

Odd thing to say. She watched him stare at the picture hanging above the fireplace and tried to start some conversation. "So, what do you do here in Hanover, Wade?"

"Teach American History at the college down the road. Civil War history to be exact. So much of it around here, you know?"

Ellie nodded. "My aunt took me to visit different battlefields when I was younger. This area was always her favorite, even when she lived in New York years ago. Mine too. Not just Gettysburg, but the whole region. I think that was behind her decision to buy this place."

"How much do you really know about it?"

"The inn? Not a lot. I mean, we shopped for many of the antiques together, and I helped her with some of the restoration work before she opened. Why?"

"The actual house itself. Not the contents so much."

She raised her eyebrows, waiting for him to get to the point.

"If you're interested in hearing about the history of the inn, Ellen, maybe you'd like to have dinner with me this weekend?"

All she could say was, "What?"

"You know, dinner. Spring break is late this year, so I'm free until Monday."

"Well…"

"It's been a few weeks now since the funeral. Been away from the inn at all?"

"Not much, now that you bring it up. I drove down to New York to resign from my job there and pack up my personal belongings. I paid the rent through the end of the month and sublet my apartment to a friend who was looking for a place."

"Pick you up at seven on Saturday." He gave a single downward nod, sending a mound of long straight hair down over his glasses, then walked over toward the door and went out without another word. It appeared he wasn't interested in what she'd been doing after all.

"Bye," Ellie called out to his back. She didn't remember saying yes to dinner.

On Saturday evening, the doorbell chimed promptly at seven. Ellie smoothed the front of her skirt, a bright yellow print that she hoped would bring a little sunshine to the damp evening. She let Wade in and retrieved her orange jacket and woven shoulder bag from the chair. Then she waited while he took a careful look around the parlor.

"Ready?" he asked, with an abrupt turn toward her.

"In a minute. First tell me what it is that you're looking for."

"What do you mean?"

"You've been here twice now, and both times you've examined every inch of this parlor as if you've never seen it before. Why?"

"I'll explain over dinner," he answered.

They drove through the center of town out to a steakhouse and settled into a booth. Across the table, Wade acted as if he were dining alone, looking everywhere else but at her. She was beginning to wonder why she was having dinner with him in the first place, but she tried not to let his preoccupation with whatever was on his mind annoy her.

Getting out of the house for the evening should be good for her, even if she spent it in bad company. Now she wasn't so sure. For a college professor he seemed uncomfortable making casual conversation. Maybe he just had trouble with people he didn't know. Maybe he wanted something but couldn't quite ask for it. Maybe he was just a jerk.

When the waiter came, she ordered a glass of merlot and he asked for a beer. Some local brew she'd never heard of.

More awkward silence. Then Ellie spoke up. "This is a lovely old town. When I visited Aunt Carolyn, we spent most of our time at the inn or at antique shops out in the country."

Wade got right to the point. "Made any decisions about the future of the inn?"

"I expect to reopen for guests two weeks from Monday," Ellie announced. "I've already gone to New York and tied up the loose ends of my life there."

"Good," he nodded. "Good. Glad you're staying."

That wasn't the reaction she was expecting from him. "I thought you were hoping I'd put the inn up for sale, so you could buy it yourself."

"Probably couldn't afford it now anyway. Not on my academic salary." He rearranged his salad, turning the lettuce pieces over one at a time with his fork, as if he expected to find a bug under one of them. "Maybe you'll let me visit occasionally?"

"Visit the house or visit me?"

"Both." Wade's nervous laughter helped to clear the air a little.

The waiter delivered their steaks and they busied themselves with making room on the table, shifting bread plates and glasses around. Wade slid a knife through his filet, stabbed the piece with his fork and gave it a thorough inspection. It must have met with his approval since he ate it and cut another. Ellie tore herself away from watching him and concentrated on her own plate.

Once satisfied that his dinner was acceptable, Wade resumed their conversation. "Did your aunt ever tell you what happened at the inn during the Civil War?"

Ellie shook her head. "She told me about the fighting here in Hanover just before the Battle of Gettysburg but that's really all. She was so excited about finding an inn for sale in such a perfect location. I can still hear the thrill in her voice that day. 'Ellie, dear, you'll never guess what I found!' I thought she was talking about a lost kitten or something." Her voice faltered as she shared the conversation with Wade. "It seems like such a short time ago that she bought the inn, and now…" She reached into her pocket for a tissue.

"The house was damaged, you know. In the fighting." Wade said, clearly interested in talking about the building and not in Aunt Carolyn or in easing Ellie's grief.

Ellie wiped away a tear and tried to focus on what he was saying, which had nothing to do with the way she was feeling. "It was the front corner, wasn't it?" she responded.

"Exactly. It happened when the original owner still lived there. That's her picture over the fireplace in your parlor." He turned his gaze toward the window with a wistful smile. "Your aunt used to let me sit in the parlor and look at that picture now and then. Long as I didn't bother the guests or anything."

"Aunt Carolyn mentioned the portrait a few times. She said it was unique."

"Isn't she beautiful? That's Sally. Sally Brendel." He spoke her name with a peculiar gleam in his eye, the way a man would introduce his bride. "The place was known as the Brendel Farm, but Sally's husband was killed early in the war. Left her with no choice but to sell off some of the land and turn the house into an inn. Hard life for a widow during those times."

"She must have been a strong woman."

"Indeed, she was. Brave, too."

"You talk about her as if you knew her."

"I did. I do. Well…"

"I don't understand."

"Sally was the closest friend of my great-great-great grand-mother, Martha Savage, before the war. My ancestors lived in Maryland then. Later moved to Virginia. All true southerners. My family saved Sally's letters. I have them now. Very fragile, so I try not to read them too often."

"Her letters? After all these years?"

Wade nodded. "My family felt sorry for Sally. First, she lost her husband in the war, then the Union Army trampled what was left of her crops and sawed branches off her fruit trees, so they could pick off all the ripe cherries and peaches. The soldiers marched in and took over her house to use as a hospital. Brought in all their dead and dying. Ripped the doors off the hinges to use for operating tables. Cut arms and legs off the wounded while they lay sprawled on top of the grand piano that Sally loved so much." He shot a dark scowl across the table as if daring her to dispute his story.

"I can't imagine what that must have been like." She tried to envision the parlor at the inn filled with bleeding men and felt a distinct chill creep across her shoulders.

"The house is only four miles from the Mason Dixon line. It was hit by a Yankee artillery shell. That's why the stone work at the side of the porch still doesn't exactly match."

"That sort of thing must have happened a lot around here in those days. I thought people could submit claims to the government after the war for the damage they incurred."

"She did!" he shouted.

People seated at nearby tables stopped their conversation to turn and look at them.

Wade was starting to embarrass her. Ellie lowered her eyes and kept them fixed on her plate, hoping he'd get the hint. She didn't intend to sit here much longer if he kept on this way. Walking out would create even more of a scene, so she hoped it wouldn't come to that. Besides, Sally's story was fascinating to her, especially if all these things really did happen at Ivy Garden. Once he launched into Sally's story, his former awkwardness disappeared. Despite Wade's peculiarities, she wanted to hear more from him.

As if he could hear her thoughts, his tone softened a little. "By the time the Army pulled out, she was so angry at the Union for everything they had done to her, she began to help the Confederacy. Running an inn so close to the state of Maryland gave her the means to stay alive by renting rooms of her house and gave her the perfect cover for passing information back and forth, especially with the help of her dear friend, Martha Savage. She hid Confederate deserters in her cellar when she had the opportunity, too. Eventually the federal government caught onto her undercover activities and refused to pay her claim, calling her a traitor to the Union."

"Then she was a criminal."

Wade glared at her, tossing his fork onto the empty plate in front of him with a clatter.

More stares from neighboring tables.

It was too late to take back her accusation but based on what he'd just said, the woman really was a criminal. "Calm down please."

He looked away.

"What happened to her?"

"Sally died a few years after the war." Wade glared intensely at Ellie to make sure she was paying attention. "Alone and bitter. In her will, she left all her earthly belongings to Martha Savage. Then the feds came along and seized the inn. Back taxes, they said. In those days, punishment for treason wasn't something they wanted to inflict on a woman, so they watched her, harassed her, and interfered in everything she tried to do. Made her life miserable."

Ellie didn't know what to say. Was she supposed to feel sorry for Sally and Martha?

"Damn Yankees," he grumbled. Wade downed the last of his beer in one big gulp, slammed the mug on the table and gave her a curt "Let's go."

During the ride home, Ellie's efforts to engage him in further conversation were met with one-word responses, so she gave up. Why was he so irritated? She had nothing to do with Sally Brendel's misery.

When they pulled up to the curb in front of the inn, she thanked him for dinner, said good night, and got out of the car with a sigh of relief. As soon as she closed the car door, he drove off with a loud squeal as if he couldn't wait to get away from her. Well, if she never saw Wade Savage again, it would be no great loss. She wasn't impressed with him but had to admit his tales about the inn and its history were intriguing.

Fumbling through her purse for the door key, she chided herself for not leaving the porch lights on. She hadn't left any lamps on inside either. Clouds drifted across the face of the full moon, masking what little light there was. The darkness gave the front of the inn an eerie, almost menacing look that she'd never seen before. She shivered.

When her fingers finally grasped the door key, she hurried up to the house. Once inside, she dropped her jacket and bag on the chair and turned on the table lamp. A prickly feeling crept up her neck. She turned around to face the fireplace.

Sally Brendel's portrait was hanging upside down.

2

Ellie stumbled backward a few steps, just far enough to put a solid wall behind her while she took a long slow look around the room. No sign of forced entry at the front of the house. Nothing missing. Windows still locked just as she left them. She listened. No sound in the house at all, except her hammering heart and ragged breathing. Nothing was out of place. Except that picture.

Unsure how long her shaky knees would support her, Ellie wanted to sink into a chair, but she was too frightened to sit down. Better to stay on her feet if she could, in case she had to start running from something.

Keeping a wary eye on the portrait, she forced herself to put one foot in front of the other and began switching on the rest of the lights in the parlor, in the dining room, and then the kitchen. The bright lights helped to calm her nerves. The house was so still. Almost too still.

She brought a chair from the dining room and placed it below the picture. Slipping off her sandals before standing on the cushion, she hesitated long enough to wipe her sweaty palms on the sides of her skirt. With slow and careful movements, Ellie balanced the edge of the frame on her knee and reached behind the picture to lift the wire off its hook. It was a lot heavier than she anticipated and it slipped. She caught it in time, but the ragged edge of the frame tore a hole in her skirt and sliced a cut in her leg, just above the kneecap. Turning the picture right side up took every bit of strength her arms could produce. She raised it back up to the hook with a grunt and after a couple of tries, felt the wire catch.

Holding her breath, she slowly released the edge of the frame, half expecting it to crash to the floor. Heart still pounding, she reached up and grasped the edges one more time to straighten it. That was when she noticed a drop of blood from the cut on her leg clinging to the bottom edge of the frame.

Ellie went into the kitchen for a wet cloth but stopped in the middle of the parlor on her way back. The cloth fell from her hand when she saw three drops of blood on the carpet near the chair she'd been standing on. Her eyes traveled upward to see a fourth about to fall from the corner of the frame. It fell, followed by another, and then another.

Looking down at the tear in her skirt, she put her finger through the hole to touch the cut. She pulled it back out and stared at her hand. It was dry.

The blood was coming right from Sally's heart. It trickled down the front of her dress to the bottom of the painting and onto the floor.

Ellie didn't know what prevented her from screaming, but no one would have heard her anyway. She ran out of the parlor, ignoring the rattling of the glass in the French doors when she slammed them shut. Making her way down the hallway, she kept looking back over her shoulder at the closed parlor doors as if she expected them to burst open again on their own.

Finally, she reached her apartment door. Once inside, she slammed it behind her, flipped the deadbolt, and switched on the overhead light, all in one motion. Ellie leaned against the door and let out the breath she'd been holding since she came home in a heavy jagged sigh.

She rubbed her fingertips across her forehead to ease the pain above her eyebrows that hadn't been there until she walked into the house. Now that the immediate crisis had passed, her body was allowing itself to react just like it did at the end of a busy shift in the Emergency Room at the hospital. With an intense headache.

Once all the lights in the apartment were on, she picked up her prescription medication for headaches like this along with a glass of water and carried them to the sitting area at the far end of the room. Facing the door with her back to the wall seemed like the safest place to sit while she tried to figure out what had happened.

In her attempt to shake two pills into her hand, she managed to scatter half the bottle onto her lap and across the floor at her feet. She picked up two of them with an unsteady hand and swallowed them. Even if they didn't help her headache, they might calm her nerves.

Ellie forced herself to relax and come up with some logical explanation for this. She wanted to believe that Aunt Carolyn's spirit lingered here, but what happened earlier was sinister. Almost evil. It had started outside with that eerie feeling before she found her keys.

A glance at the clock radio on the nightstand in the next room startled her. Two hours had passed. She still hadn't been able to come up with a logical explanation. Her conclusions were few and not very sound, but something Wade had said to her kept coming back to her. She was beginning to wonder what he really meant when he told her he knew Sally Brendel.

She considered calling Wade, but she didn't have his number. Besides, was she ready to confide in him about this anyway? After the way he talked at dinner, she didn't think so. Too late to call the neighbors. The Kellers had told her several times to come over if she ever needed them for anything, but Ellie doubted they had ghost hunting in mind.

Those bloodstains in the carpet would set if she didn't scrub them out soon. Replacing the parlor carpet wasn't part of her plan. She'd have to go back out there and take care of it. Then there was the matter of the front door. She didn't remember locking it behind her when she came in. Bad enough that it had only one bolt. Her apartment in New York had three and securing all of them was the first thing she did every time she walked in. Ellie was not about to leave this door unlocked. Not tonight.

The entire time she'd been sitting here, her ears hadn't picked up a single sound that might have come from the parlor. During the weeks that Ellie had spent here alone, the silence never bothered her. She found it a relaxing contrast to the bustle of the city. This was a different kind of silence and it set her on edge.

The battle between her fear of the unknown and the lure of the unlocked door raged on. In the end, she knew there was no choice. She'd have to go back and lock the front door. So, the journey began, one hesitant step at a time.

The lights were still on just as she'd left them. In fact, the parlor was the same as she'd left it before she went out with Wade. Everything in its place. Ellie's eyes moved from the portrait down to the carpet.

No blood stains.

Fear sent a cold punch through Ellie's stomach. Panting, she dropped to her knees below the picture, and ran her hand over the carpet. It was dry and spotless.

Using both hands, she pressed her frantic fingertips deep into the fibers and pulled them apart, looking for some sign of the bloodstains she knew had been there. The carpet was clean.

Up on her feet, she ran a tentative finger along the bottom of the frame first, then up the sides. Every part of the frame she touched felt dry. No sign of blood anywhere. She pulled the picture away from the wall far enough to look behind it and ran her hand along the painted surface. Nothing there either.

With her back against the opposite wall, she studied the picture. Sally's face wore a hint of a smile that Ellie hadn't noticed before. A faint expression of…what was it? Satisfaction?

Enough of this. Bolting the front door, she decided to leave all the lights on until morning, just in case. In case of what, she had no idea, but it seemed like the prudent thing to do under the circumstances.

That was when she heard it. A man's voice. Somewhat muffled but speaking to her. Using her name. The voice interrupted her thoughts the way the loudspeaker in the grocery store cuts off the music and announces, "Cleanup on aisle nine." But it was inside her head.

Please do not worry, Ellen. Sally is just a bit angry right now. She does not want you here.

Her head whipped around, scanning every corner of the room, but no one was there. "Who is it?" she called out. "Who's there?"

Silence.

25

Nothing she said or did brought back the voice she knew she'd heard.

After a fitful night of restless sleep, Ellie awoke with a throbbing head. Pain crawled from the back of her neck over the crown of her head and down to the bridge of her nose. She sat up in bed and then lay down again, reluctant to venture beyond the covers. At least she didn't have to go very far for another dose of pain medication. It was still all over the floor.

A steamy shower followed by strong coffee and some toast helped Ellie regain her practical perspective. Broad daylight was a big step in the right direction too. A beautiful Sunday like this should not be wasted over something that was evidently nothing more than a bad dream. In an hour, she felt much better.

All three of the inn's employees had been on paid vacation since Aunt Carolyn died. Alice the housekeeper, Martha the cook and Fred the handyman were all very grateful for her generosity. Each of the them had stopped by now and then since the funeral to see how she was doing and to ask if she needed anything. They were thrilled when she told them she had decided to reopen the inn on May 1 and all three promised to report back to work in plenty of time to have everything ready for the first guest to arrive.

Ellie spent the rest of the morning at the computer to catch up on business details and to notify everyone on the inn's mailing list about the reopening. Then she went outside to see what needed to be done about the grounds around the inn.

Car keys in hand, Ellie walked all the way around the inn, making a mental note of the condition of the flower beds before heading out to the garden center. She'd spent enough time inside lately and digging in the soil could often be therapeutic. It would give her an opportunity to think and she'd accomplish something in the process.

She returned with a carload of potting soil, fertilizer, and trays of petunias and pansies in assorted colors. The mature lilac bush that she couldn't pass up filled the entire back of her SUV with leaves, branches, and an intoxicating fragrance.

Tackling the toughest job first, Ellie assembled the garden tools she'd carried from the barn and began to dig a hole for the lilac at the back of the house where she could see it from the kitchen window. She pictured her guests relaxing on the bench next to the ivy covered back wall of the inn, admiring the purple blossoms in the spring.

No, Ellen. Not here. It belongs in the front of the house. At the corner.

There was no mistaking that voice. It was the same one she'd heard last night. The shovel fell from her hand and she turned. This time she wasn't surprised to find no one there. The voice didn't make her feel threatened or afraid, although she couldn't say why. Whoever it was clearly didn't want her to plant the lilac in this spot and Ellie wasn't about to argue with a spirit whose mind was made up. She retrieved her shovel and filled in the hole, her thoughts filled with Sally Brendel and the unknown man behind the voice.

Ellie moved everything out to the front of the house and began to dig again. In her mind, she went over her conversation with Wade one more time but couldn't recall any mention of a specific man in the inn's past. It was all about Sally.

First thing tomorrow, she'd go down to the Hanover library or visit the historical society. Maybe she could learn something about the house and its former occupants that might help her identify the voice. Besides, her guests would surely ask questions about the history of the house and she wanted to be able to tell them more than the things she'd learned from Wade.

By late afternoon, the lilac bush graced the front corner of the house and a thick row of petunias lined each side of the driveway. With the loose dirt swept from the pavement, and all her tools and supplies put back in the barn, Ellie took one more walk across the front lawn to enjoy her sense of accomplishment. The inn had come alive.

A voice called to her from across the yard. She looked up to see Myra Keller approaching. "My, you've been working hard today, dear! Come on over and have yourself a glass of lemonade with George and me."

"Oh thanks, Myra, but maybe another time. I'm covered with dirt." Once Ellie had finished working, the fatigue she'd been ignoring began to settle in, and she was looking forward to a hot soak in the tub and a glass of wine.

"Nonsense. We'll sit outside on the porch. I baked an apple pie this afternoon. I was just getting ready to cut it."

"You convinced me," Ellie said with a smile. Never able to refuse a slice of Myra's pie since the day Aunt Carolyn moved in, she followed her neighbor across the grassy field that separated the two houses.

Smaller than Ivy Garden, the Keller house was still too large for George and Myra now that their five children had grown up and left the nest, but they were determined to live out their lives here. The elderly couple began treating Ellie like an adopted daughter since Aunt Carolyn died and although she was grateful for their kindness, at times their attention bordered on smothering. She hoped today wasn't one of those times.

Settled on the porch swing, Ellie held out her hands to accept a large slice of apple pie that almost hung over the edges of the plate. A melting mound of vanilla ice cream covered the top crust. She closed her eyes and inhaled the aroma of cinnamon and nutmeg before taking the first bite.

"Delicious as always, Myra. Thank you."

"Just an everyday pie."

"Are you getting along all right over there by yourself, Ellie?" asked George. "You know we're right here if you ever need anything."

"Yes, and I really appreciate that. I'm doing okay, but sure do miss Aunt Carolyn." She hesitated, then said, "You know this probably sounds strange, but sometimes it just seems like she's still there in a way. Know what I mean?"

Ellie couldn't be certain, but it seemed like Myra's fork slowed its approach to her mouth as she and George exchanged knowing glances. They acted as if each were waiting for the other to respond but neither one did.

The siren from the town fire truck would have drowned out their voices anyway. It roared past the house followed by the Sheriff's car, more sirens and flashing lights.

"Wonder what's going on?" mumbled George through a mouthful of pie. "Looks like they're headed away from town." He checked his watch. "Well, it'll probably be on the evening news." Myra and George watched the news on television twice a day, every day. Noon and six. They never missed it, according to Aunt Carolyn.

They watched a thickening cloud of smoke rise above the trees in the distance and speculated about what could be burning but came to no firm conclusion.

"By the way," Myra said, "I happened to see you go out with that history professor last night."

Ellie groaned.

"Wade Savage," Myra added as if she thought Ellie was unsure which history professor she was talking about.

"We had dinner, yes. He told me some of the history of the inn."

"I'd be careful about him, if I were you, Ellie." George set his plate on the small end table and leaned forward in his chair, elbows on his knees.

"Why do you say that?"

"He's what you might call eccentric."

That wasn't one of the words Ellie would have picked to describe Wade. "He seemed very interested in Ivy Garden."

"Wade always was," said George. "No doubt about that. Did he tell you about trying to buy the place?"

Ellie nodded.

"See, Wade has this...oh, I guess you'd have to call it an obsession with the inn. Mostly with the widow Brendel. She was the original owner of the place, you know."

Now it was Ellie's turn to wear the expression of suppressed information. She couldn't bring herself to share the strange occurrences with Sally's portrait. Not that she expected her neighbors to think she was crazy, but she hadn't quite sorted it out for herself yet.

She hadn't even decided to share it with Wade. He seemed very interested in what happened to Sally from a historical perspective, but Ellie wouldn't call him obsessed. Truth was, she really didn't know Wade very well at all. Evidently the Kellers did.

"Well, you know, it was just a first date. Not even really a date exactly."

"Whatever it was, dear, George is just telling you to be a little careful. That's all." She snapped her fingers. "Say, how would you like to meet my nephew sometime? He lives here in town and I think he'd really like you."

"I appreciate it, Myra, but I'm really not looking for anyone right now. I'm still getting settled and have a lot to do." She set her plate down on the table. "Thanks for the pie. I'd better get going."

George glanced down at his watch. "Time for the news anyway. Maybe we'll find out what all the ruckus was about."

Rested and refreshed after an uneventful night, Ellie arrived at the library early Monday morning, soon after it opened. The librarian introduced her to an extensive selection of books on local history and an even bigger collection of old newspapers, scanned and electronically available. Impressive for a small town. Research on the internet would have been a lot easier, but there wasn't enough detailed local information available on the web. Not the kind she was looking for, anyway. She would have to learn about Sally Brendel and the man behind the mysterious voice the hard way. One page at a time.

The morning flew by as Ellie immersed herself in the past. She learned a lot about the battle that took place near the inn, the units that fought here and the devastating effects on the town, but nothing that would help explain what had happened in her parlor.

By early afternoon, she couldn't ignore her growling stomach any longer. Time to get something to eat. After applying for a library card, she checked out as many books as she could carry. One book went into her bag and the rest onto the front seat of the car. Then she headed down to a coffee shop that served sandwiches.

An unexpected ache of sadness caught her off guard when she remembered that the last time she'd been there was with

Aunt Carolyn. They had just picked out some fabric to sew new curtains for some of the guest rooms and decided to stop there for a bite to eat.

Ellie ordered a tuna salad on wheat at the counter and carried her coffee over to an empty table. The library book that she had tucked into her bag beckoned and she pulled it out. No sooner had she opened the cover than she heard someone call to her.

"I thought that was you!"

"Hi Fran!"

"I felt so bad when I heard about your aunt. You know, she was one of the nicest people I ever interviewed for the newspaper. I'm sorry I couldn't make it to the funeral. When she bought Ivy Garden, she just welcomed me in to do her story as if she'd been giving interviews all her life. Made my job so much easier."

Ellie responded with a bittersweet smile. "Are you having lunch? How about joining me?" She moved her jacket from the opposite chair and made room on the table. While Fran got settled with her food, Ellie went over to the counter to pick up her own sandwich.

Fran didn't waste any time catching up. "I haven't seen any For Sale signs out at the inn. Are you planning to stay?"

"Yes. I have guests lined up starting on the first of next month. It may take a little while to get into the routine of things, but Aunt Carolyn was a good teacher."

"You probably have a lot to do, taking care of things and getting ready to reopen the inn, but please don't be a stranger. It would be great to see more of your face around town."

"Once I get caught up, I expect to be out and about more." Ellie liked Fran ever since the day they'd met more than three years ago. There was nothing pretentious about her and she was so easy to talk to. That's probably why she was so good at her job as a journalist. People just naturally wanted to tell her things.

"If you want to run a Grand Reopening sort of ad in the paper, just give me a call."

"I hadn't really thought about it. I'll let you know."

"Good. Now, I've got to ask. Was that you I saw in the car with Wade Savage driving through town the other night?"

Don't people in this town have anything to do except watch her? Ellie's expression must have given away her thoughts.

"Sorry. I didn't mean to sound nosy. I was just leaving the newspaper office when I saw you go by."

"No, it's okay. It's just that you're the second person to mention Wade to me. I only went out to dinner once. One date." Again Ellie found herself saying, "Not even really a date."

"Going out on a dinner date isn't what's causing the buzz. It's who you were with."

"Okay. I'll admit Wade's a little odd in some ways, but he's not the worst man I've ever been out with. He told me a lot of interesting things about the history of the inn." Ellie put the rest of her sandwich down and picked up her coffee mug. She was starting to lose her appetite.

"Look, this is going to be in tomorrow's edition of the paper anyway, so I may as well tell you."

"Tell me what?"

"Wade was burned in an explosion yesterday. He's in the hospital."

The news caught her in mid swallow and she almost choked.

"You okay?"

Ellie nodded. "I think so. Is he all right? What happened?"

"He'll recover. The burns aren't too bad, but they're all over his body. Not just his hands or his face. Everywhere. What kind of fire gives somebody the same light toasting on every square inch?" Fran leaned across the table and lowered her voice. "Listen, you haven't gone over to his place, have you?"

"No. As I said, I only went out with him once. He picked me up, we ate at the steakhouse and he dropped me off afterwards. That was it. Why?"

"Well, the details are still kind of sketchy but according to the police report, he was in that workshop he has in the barn behind his house out by the cemetery. He built some kind of machine out there and I guess it just blew up. The police couldn't figure out exactly what it was or what Wade was doing when it happened. The strangest thing is that Wade isn't talking. He won't tell anyone what he was working on. Not the police, not the fire department, not the doctor at the hospital.

He says he didn't commit any crime since it happened on his own property and they don't need to know anything. He claims he's just a history professor and not some top-secret scientist."

"Well, I don't know him very well, but he did seem like a rather private individual."

"Ellie, the man's a fanatic. He's obsessed with Sally Brendel."

That word again. Obsessed. "Are you trying to tell me you think that Wade's interest in Sally had something to do with this explosion?"

"He wouldn't admit it when I tried to talk to him, but yes, I do. Ellie, I've lived in Hanover all my life. I went to school with him. Even when we were kids, he hung around that old stone house by himself before it became an inn. It was creepy." She looked away, then back at Ellie. "It still is."

They walked out of the coffee shop together, exchanging promises to get together again soon. Once Ellie was back in the car, her curiosity got the best of her and she drove around the area by the cemetery until she saw the smoky remains of a barn. Unlike other burned out buildings, it was impossible to determine exactly where in the barn the fire had started. The entire structure was evenly scorched. Strange.

The inn reopened with all of Aunt Carolyn's staff back at work. Alice had polished every inch of the place into a spotless but inviting glow while Martha had refilled the pantry and made up breakfast menus for the coming week. Fred scolded her for putting all those plants in by herself without calling him for help, but at the same time he seemed to recognize her need to do it. He was satisfied when she told him there were still some left for him to put in the planters around the patio. With the lawn cut and the hedges trimmed, Ivy Garden belonged on a magazine cover.

All five rooms were filled each weekend for the next month, and some of her guests even extended their stay an extra night. Ellie was developing a routine and feeling more comfortable in her new role every day. Generating a strong cash flow also helped to boost her morale. Maybe she could do this on her own after all.

Families with children under twelve were discouraged, both in the fine print of her advertising and in phone inquiries. As much as she hated to turn away a paying guest, she couldn't afford the potential damage to the costly restoration and irreplaceable antiques. One family, however, succeeded in convincing her that their ten-year-old son, who loved Civil War history, wouldn't be a problem. They wanted to stay for an entire week as soon as school was out in early June. When they offered a sizable deposit to cover any mishaps, Ellie gave in.

Upon Todd's arrival, Ellie admitted to his parents that he did indeed seem much more mature than his ten years. Polite and well behaved, Todd treated Ellie and the inn with respect. Until he became acquainted with the Kellers' visiting grandson, that is. Before long, Todd was out climbing trees with his new pal while his parents were relaxing in the rocking chairs on the front porch. The other guests were out for the day and the inn was quiet.

A piercing scream sent Ellie running from the kitchen. Todd's parents raced around the outside of the house and followed at her heels. They found Todd flat on the ground under an old oak at the back of the property. A dead limb had snapped, taking the boy down with it. He'd landed on one of the branches, putting a long gash in his left arm.

Ellie's nursing instincts took over in an instant. After making sure he had no broken bones, she helped him to his feet and led all three of them back inside to her apartment. The Kellers' grandson had disappeared, probably hoping to escape any blame for the accident.

Todd's parents were no help at all. His mother swooned at the sight of blood while his father paced the hallway outside Ellie's bathroom, more angry with his son's behavior than concerned for his well-being. Ellie recognized what was coming when Todd groaned, and his hand moved from his white face down to his stomach. She held his head while he vomited, relieved they had made it all the way to her bathroom before the nausea kicked in. Unlike most boys, he clearly wasn't accustomed to this sort of thing and it upset him.

After he had calmed down, Ellie explained to the parents that their son needed stitches and recommended that they take him to the hospital. The father balked at this idea, insisting that his son was just making a fuss and wasn't hurt that badly. Ellie envisioned the scar that would be left on the boy's arm and told them that if they refused to take him to be seen by a doctor, she would be willing to stitch it up herself. Good thing she'd recently checked to make sure the inn's blanket liability insurance was paid up.

She retrieved her medical kit from the bedroom closet and asked the parents to wait on the porch. Once she and Todd were alone, he started to relax a little. She gave him a hug, reassured him everything would be all right and explained how she would go about taking care of his arm. Only if he agreed though, because he was in charge of this. No one else. He stretched his arm out on the edge of the sink in response.

Bent over his wound, she concentrated on cleaning and closing the cut, intent on minimizing the boy's discomfort. A sudden sense of another presence caught her off guard. The gauze fell from her hand. When she turned to see who was standing at her right shoulder, breathing into her ear, no one was there.

"What's the matter?" Todd asked her. "You look funny."

"I'm all right. It's just…" Then she heard it. The same soft, kind voice of the man she could not see.

Ellen. Please, can you help my men?

3

Who could be asking for her help with his men? She had to find out. Ellie searched through every bit of information she could lay her hands on. She'd had read through everything the library had about local history, reading several pages in some books while only flipping through others. Each one brought her to the same disappointing conclusion. Authors analyzed strategic military maneuvers in immense detail but glossed over descriptions of civilians and their homes that might mention her mysterious visitor.

Wade Savage was shaping up to be her sole source of information, but she wasn't ready to go to him with her questions. Not yet, anyway. She wanted to give him plenty of time to heal from the burns he sustained from whatever that explosion was all about. Better to continue trying to learn everything there was to learn about this house and its inhabitants on her own before asking him.

She stopped in the newspaper office to see Fran, hoping she was not out on an assignment. They'd grown closer since Ellie moved to Hanover and their friendship helped ease Ellie's transition from big city nurse to small town innkeeper.

Fran jumped out of her chair to give Ellie a big hug. "What brings you here, girlfriend? How good it is to see you! You look great! Everything running smoothly at the inn? Are you ready to run that ad in the paper? Do you have time for coffee?"

Ellie laughed. "One question at a time. First, I'd love some coffee. Let's go across the street. Then we'll tackle the rest."

After getting settled at a corner table, they ironed out details of a newspaper ad for the inn. Ellie liked Fran's idea of running it in the Gettysburg paper as well but agreed to it only if Fran promised to charge her the same as any other customer.

When Ellie told her about all the flowers she'd planted, Fran offered to come by the day after tomorrow to take some photos for the ad. "No matter what anybody says," Fran told her, "A picture is still worth a thousand words." Ellie added an item to the running list in her cell phone reminding her to update the inn's tri-fold glossy brochure and print more copies. She didn't want to run out before summer was over.

"Fran, is there anything else about the inn that you know but haven't told me?"

"Like what?"

"Like who lived there besides Sally." Ellie paused. "Who might still be living there."

"I don't understand what you mean. You're the only one who lives there. As for Sally, she's been dead for at least a hundred years. Are you talking about a ghost or something? Are things going bump in the night?" Fran teased with an elbow toward Ellie's ribs. "Maybe you should have your handyman check things out."

Ellie was afraid this conversation might be a mistake, but it was too late to back away. "It's not really noises. It's more like voices."

"You mean you think the inn is haunted? Sorry Ellie. I don't think I can help you with this. I'm not into spooky stuff, even though the ghost hunters around here talk about it a lot."

"It's okay. It's just that there's just not much information anywhere about the history of the inn besides what Wade told me. He said it was Sally's farm and the Union Army used it for a hospital during the Civil War. Do you know anything more than that? About any particular people?"

"No, I really don't. You said you've been to the Hanover library. What about the York County History Center or the Adams County Historical Society? Their archives are huge."

"I called both and talked to some very nice people, but nobody gave me anything helpful."

"What about the people who owned the inn before Carolyn bought it?"

"The Kellers told me to look into that, but I had no luck tracking them down either."

"The Kellers, huh? They're always the first on the scene when something reportable happens around here, but then it always turns out they don't really know anything. They just don't want to miss a chance to spread gossip."

"That's the impression I've always had. Nice people. Just way too curious."

Fran glanced at her watch. "I've got to run. I hate to say this, but Wade probably knows more about the inn than anybody."

"That's what I was afraid you'd say."

The summer flew by and Ivy Garden continued to maintain a solid reputation based on word of mouth recommendations, magazine reviews and travel service advice. Rooms were filled into September and guests checked out with promises to return. Aunt Carolyn would be proud.

After Labor Day weekend, Ellie reviewed the reservations calendar. Still no bookings at all for next Wednesday. Instead of the tension she used to feel when a room went without a guest for a night, she now marveled at her relief to find a day with no reservations at all, so she could have some time for herself.

She'd hoped to discover something that might reveal the identity of the man behind the voice but had no luck. Although she hadn't heard his voice for several weeks, her determination to identify him had not diminished.

Ellie's last hope involved searching through the part of the attic that she and Aunt Carolyn had never found time to investigate. Maybe something that once belonged to Sally still lay hidden there and had somehow been overlooked by Wade's family long ago.

When Wednesday finally arrived, Ellie helped her staff clear away the breakfast remains. She finished the checkout paperwork for their remaining guests and prepared for the next day's arrivals. Martha, Alice, and Fred all were surprised and delighted to have the rest of the day off with pay. Ellie sent them on their way before the wall clock struck eleven.

Bright sun glowed through the east windows, promising a warm fall day. Ellie changed into denim shorts and a red sleeveless blouse. With a water bottle in the one hand, a flashlight in the other, and a tablet tucked under her arm with a pen in her pocket, she trudged up the attic steps. Why make a second trip if she could manage to carry everything at once?

At the top of the stairway, she paused long enough to flip the light switch with her elbow. The overhead light appeared to be working but didn't illuminate much of the corner where she had hoped to work. When she thought about it, that was another reason she and Aunt Carolyn had left that area of the narrow attic alone. Too hard to reach and too dimly lit, even with the flashlight she'd brought with her.

Not to be put off by a little darkness this time, Ellie went downstairs and brought back the biggest brightest light she could find in the barn. She held it up at her shoulder and stepped around the old trunk, bending low to avoid hitting her head.

Suddenly the air in the attic turned heavy and thick. It wasn't from the heat or the dust. Ellie felt surrounded by an energy that made every hair on her body stand up, like static electricity only stronger. This was not the spirit of Aunt Carolyn and Ellie knew it. It wasn't the cold chill that swirled around her when Sally was present either. This felt different.

Drawn further into the corner by a pull she couldn't explain, she lifted her light higher and stepped around a stack of boxes toward a faint glow under the eaves. The energy behind it drew her closer, as if something or someone wanted her to follow.

The glow was coming from the floor under a small table covered with a pile of old bedding. She slid the table aside, exposing an oblong wooden box between the joists at the edge of the floorboards. As soon as she uncovered the box and touched it, the glow disappeared.

Cradling it in both hands, Ellie lifted it out of its hiding place. The wooden box was heavy and awkward, but she managed to carry it to the other side of the attic where the light was better. Crouching over it, she blew on the lid, scattering the dust from the surface and revealing the familiar Union Army insignia that she had seen in books.

The most intriguing part of the box was the set of initials carved in the lid. With her fingertip, she traced the letters:

G.F.A. Leaving behind everything she'd brought with her, she brought the box downstairs.

In the parlor, she opened the blind behind her favorite chair to let the sunlight in over her shoulder and sat down. Balancing the box on her knees, she tried to open the broken clasp but found it had become embedded in the wood. With a dull table knife from the kitchen, she began to pry it apart in slow and gentle movements. When it came loose, Ellie held her breath and opened the lid.

The box contained the oldest surgical instruments she'd ever seen. Each compartment inside was lined with dark red velvet. Scalpels, syringes, tubing, small clamps and tourniquets, scissors, a surgical saw and a few items she couldn't identify. All of them stained with blood that had long since turned black. Her hand moved toward the largest scalpel and lifted it gently out of its resting place. It felt warm in her hand, radiating a soft but distinct crackle of energy.

A movement in the parlor mirror caught her attention and she almost dropped the scalpel. More than a wisp of white this time. A shifting mist, wavy and silvery, became clear enough for Ellie to make out a man's face. He had a short gray beard mixed with white and wavy gray hair that curled along the collar of a Union officer's uniform jacket.

Do you understand now why I need you to help my men?

It was the same voice she'd heard before. Peering into the mirror, she tried to make out more details in the face of the man who spoke to her. He had the saddest eyes she'd ever seen. Curious but unafraid, she responded in a soft gentle voice. "Who are you?"

Dr. Grant Alexander. Major. Union Officer in the Army of the Potomac.

She glanced down quickly at the lid of the box and back up to the image in the mirror, afraid it might disappear if her eyes left it for too long. "G.F.A.," she whispered. "These are your instruments, aren't they?"

Yes, Ellen.

The phone rang, bringing the bizarre encounter to an abrupt ending. The image disappeared. Reluctant to let him go, her eyes strained to find some remnant of what she had just seen but he was gone. Not even a shadow remained.

Lowering the box gently to the floor beside her chair, Ellie had no doubt that she had just carried on a conversation with a ghost. It bewildered her, but she wasn't frightened. In fact, she was disappointed that it ended as quickly as it began.

She felt as if she'd just awoken from a deep sleep. The phone's persistent ringing put life back into her feet and she made her way to the desk. The red light on the phone indicating a voice mail was waiting blinked at her. One thing at a time. Pick up the phone first.

"Ivy Garden Inn. Good Afternoon." Was she slurring?

"Is that you, Ellie? You sound kind of strange. Are you all right?" Fran wasn't one to beat round the bush.

"I think so." Her own voice sounded strange to her. She cleared her throat. "I don't know."

"What is it?"

"Hard to say. I just..." How could she begin to explain this, even if her head wasn't full of cotton?

"Look, I'm going to lock up here at the newspaper and I'll be right over."

"It's okay, Fran. I'm all right. Just a little..."

"A little what?"

"I'm not sure."

"Ten minutes," Fran said and hung up the phone.

Ellie returned to her chair in the parlor and brought the box back onto her lap. The only thing she could see in the mirror now was the clear reflection of the other side of the room. No hint that anything else had ever appeared there. She ran her finger across the initials in the lid of the box and whispered, "Grant Alexander." She repeated his name a second time, a little louder. No response.

"Snap out of it," she scolded herself out loud. "Did you really think you could conjure up a spirit on demand?" The dreamy fog that had descended on her during that strange conversation was fading now, leaving her feeling stronger and more alert.

Fran's rusted Oldsmobile roared into the driveway, still in need of the new muffler she kept planning to have installed but couldn't quite get around to taking care of. Ellie opened the door before her friend reached the front steps. "Hi, Fran. Don't look so worried. I'm really fine."

"You look better than you sounded on the phone. What's going on?"

"Come on inside." Ellie held the door, and then followed Fran into the parlor.

"Feel anything?" Ellie asked.

"Like what?"

"Anything."

"No. What's the matter with you?"

"Can you stay a while? I'll open a bottle of wine."

"Sure." Fran shrugged and followed Ellie into the kitchen, making no effort to conceal the frown of concern on her face. She pulled out a wooden chair and sat with her elbows on the table, chin on her fists, watching Ellie pull an Italian red from the small wine rack and uncork it. "One favor, please," she said, accepting the full stemmed glass Ellie handed her. "Start from the very beginning of whatever this is about, okay?"

Ellie did.

By the time they finished analyzing all the strange occurrences at the inn since Aunt Carolyn's funeral, the sky outside the kitchen window had grown dark. The last slice of the pepperoni pizza delivered earlier had grown cold. So had Fran. She kept shivering and rubbing her arms, remarking "Oh, that gives me the chills," as Ellie continued to recount the details of one experience after the next.

"I hope you don't think I'm crazy. Every word of this is the absolute truth, I swear."

"Oh, I believe you, Ellie. Don't ever doubt that. Just be careful, okay? Especially where Sally's concerned. A spirit with a grudge to carry is nothing you want to mess around with."

Ellie nodded. "Okay."

"Now, can I see that box of instruments?"

"Yes. It's out in the parlor." Ellie left the kitchen, expecting Fran to follow right behind her. She turned around to see her friend still seated at the table.

"Could we look at it here in the kitchen and not in the parlor?" Fran asked, pulling her sweater tightly around her. "Sally's portrait gives me the willies."

The meek tone in her voice surprised Ellie. From the stories Fran had shared since they'd known each other, she'd gotten herself into some pretty rough situations in order to get a story for the paper. None of them seemed to put fear into her the way Sally did.

"Of course. I'll bring it," Ellie replied over her shoulder. Passing by the desk, Ellie noticed the red light on the phone still blinking in the dark with the message she'd never picked up. Innkeeping 101: Return phone calls promptly. An ignored message could result in a missed reservation. She played the message with the speaker on.

Listening to the familiar voice, the two women exchanged glances, first of surprise, then concern.

"Hello. Ellie. Wade Savage here." A pause. "Need to talk to you. Wondered if I might borrow the portrait. Sally's portrait." Another pause followed by some throat clearing. "Just for a short time. Expect to return it, of course." He left his phone number and hung up.

"What would he want with the portrait?" Ellie asked. "He could look at it here if he wanted to see it again."

"I have no idea. He must have seen it a gazillion times already."

"Remember the fire at his place last spring?"

"Sure I do." Fran frowned as she worked at making a connection between that and the phone message but couldn't.

"Suppose he was trying to make some kind of psychic contact with Sally. If I can feel electrical energy when the spirits are near, maybe he can too. Maybe that's what caused the explosion."

"I never heard of ghosts blowing things up."

"I'm not saying the ghosts did it. Maybe it was something he was doing to try to reach them. Or reach Sally. I don't know."

They mulled this over, both coming up with possible reasons behind Wade's strange request, then dismissing them as ridiculous.

Back at the kitchen table huddled over the box, Ellie showed her friend the surgical instruments one at a time. They felt warm and alive in her hand. She thought of the stories that must lie buried inside every item she held.

Together they emptied the box all the way down to the fragile rolls of muslin bandages and wooden spools of silk thread. "Imagine what it must have been like to operate on somebody with tools like this," marveled Fran. "Unbelievable." She handed the last scalpel back to Ellie, who repacked the box exactly as she'd found it.

"Maybe it's time to capitalize on the fact that Ivy Garden had once been a Civil War hospital," Fran suggested, bringing Ellie back to the 21st century.

"What do you mean?"

"You could display these instruments in a case on the wall above the piano, right where they had been used over 150 years ago. A treasure like this would enhance the historical charm of this place. This kind of thing makes for good advertising."

"You know, that's not a bad idea. After all, this box is part of the inn's past. To tell you the truth, I wasn't sure what to do with it. I'd never sell it and I sure don't want to just pack it away where I found it."

"You'd have to find the right person to clean these things up and restore them without changing their authenticity in any way. Know what I mean?"

"Hmm. I think I may know of someone who can help. He's a retired physician who studies Civil War medicine. Wonderful man. He's been a guest here several times and knows a lot of people. In fact, I remember seeing him in the reservation system, so he's made arrangements to return to the inn. I just don't remember exactly when."

"He sounds like a good place to start."

They cleaned up the remains of their dinner, hastily set aside earlier to make room on the kitchen table for the box and its contents.

"Thanks for the pizza and salad. You didn't have to buy."

"Don't mention it," Ellie replied with a wave of her hand. She held up the bottle of wine they had opened earlier and said, "There's a glass left in here for each of us. Let's finish it."

She refilled their glasses while Fran picked up the dishcloth and wiped off the countertop. "I'm still climbing out of the hole in my bank account since the divorce," she said, scrubbing harder and harder. "It's been a year since I threw the bum out and the bills keep coming. I can't even scrape enough together to get the car fixed."

"Starting over on your own is so hard. Not only financially, but emotionally too."

"You sound like you've been there, even though I know you haven't."

"No I haven't, but I've had friends who went through the same thing you're facing. No matter what the circumstances, everyone I've known who's been divorced takes a long time to recover. But they all survived, and you will too."

"I'd like to believe that."

"No reason not to."

"You're such an optimist. How come you never got married? You've dated plenty of men. Look at you. Long curly hair, knockout blue eyes. Willowy shape to die for. Besides being beautiful, you're smart and fun to be with."

She gave Fran's arm a teasing shove. "Come on now."

"No, I'm serious. Why not?"

"Well, I used to think it was my work, you know? Too busy to get serious with anyone. My schedule at the hospital was always crazy, switching shifts, getting called in at the last minute when somebody didn't show up for work or putting in overtime on nights when the Emergency Room was filled with critical cases."

"I can see how that sort of thing can get in the way of a romantic relationship but if you really want to be with someone..."

"It was intense, stressful work, Fran. I'd come home after a long shift totally drained, worrying about what I could have done that might have changed the outcome for someone. I had nothing left to give to a relationship."

"Or maybe you just never met the right man."

They were both quiet for a moment and Ellie thought about men she'd met, dated, and then lost interest in.

Fran rambled on about the late hour and all the things she had to do tomorrow. "Before I leave though, we need to decide what to do about Wade wanting Sally's portrait."

Ellie slumped in her chair. "I'd like to just forget he even called but he doesn't seem like the type who will take no for an answer."

"He's definitely not." Fran pushed her empty glass aside and leaned across the table. She held out her fingers one at a time while she explained her friend's options. "Now, the way

I see it, you've got three choices: One, you ignore his phone call. If he calls again, say you never got the message. That will just delay things, but you could do it. Two, you call him back and tell him the portrait stays here. He can look at it, but he can't take it. Or three, you let him borrow it."

"I like the first choice the best, even though I know ignoring his phone call won't make him go away."

"Think about it, Ellie. You don't want him breaking in here and taking it, do you?"

"He wouldn't do anything like that."

"I wouldn't be too sure." Fran carried her glass over to the sink and set it down. She turned around and leaned against the dishwasher with her arms folded. "About five years ago, Wade Savage was arrested for breaking and entering. He was found guilty."

Ellie gasped. She moved her mouth to speak but couldn't make any words come out.

Fran continued as if she hadn't noticed Ellie's reaction. "Public information. We printed it on the 'Police Page'. He later returned the goods and paid the fine. The judge was a friend of the family and the whole thing was later wiped from the books."

"What…what did he steal?" Ellie couldn't believe this.

"Never could dig up any details on that. I only know he broke into an antique shop. One of those renovated brick storefronts in the center of town. It went out of business a while back."

Ellie hadn't considered that Wade was capable of such a thing until Fran told her this. Now she was beginning to wonder what else he might do, given his obsession with Sally. "Fran, maybe we'd better hide the portrait. Just in case. Not just because it's probably worth a lot of money, but I think it has some kind of mystical power."

"I never liked the way that woman glares at me anyway. Got anything else to hang in its place until this blows over?"

"I'm sure I can find something. Will you help me?"

"What are friends for?" Fran put on a brave front as she marched into the parlor and headed toward the fireplace with Ellie right behind her. "Wait a minute," she said, turning around. "Before we tackle this, let's figure out where we're going to put it. That thing's got to be heavy. It's not something we want to lug all over the house while we decide. Maybe there's a closet or something with a lock on it?"

Ellie thought for a moment. "There's a storage area off the back hall with a skeleton key in the keyhole. It's kind of out of the way. Guests don't use it and I haven't found a need for it myself. There's not much in it."

"Sounds like the right place. Let's have a look."

Ellie turned on the lights in the back hall, opened the door to the storage area, and tested the lock. Satisfied that the key worked, she stepped inside and pulled the cord dangling next to a single bare light bulb. It shed enough light to confirm that there was plenty of space inside for the portrait, along with a large dried flower arrangement that they could hang in its place.

When they returned to the parlor, Ellie noticed the wall above the portrait glistened, like it was wet. She went over and touched the painted surface. It was soaked. Above her head, a steady stream of water trickled down the entire width of the wall from a huge dark spot on the ceiling starting at the hallway.

"Dealing with leaky plumbing was not on my agenda. Especially with new guests arriving tomorrow." Ellie dashed out to the desk and picked up the phone to call Fred, the handyman. So much for the light giddy feeling the last glass of wine had given her. Reality crashed down with a vengeance all too soon.

Fran came up from behind her and took the phone out of her hand. "Wait a minute," she said, her speech a little thick. "What could be leaking? No one's been upstairs for what ... almost twelve hours?" Thick speech or not, Fran's thinking was sharper than her own.

"You're right." Ellie stared at her. "None of the bathrooms are directly above that spot either."

They looked at the ceiling and then at each other before Fran spoke the obvious question out loud.

"So then…where is this water coming from?" Her voice trembled.

"I don't know." Ellie put the phone back in its cradle, trying to keep her own voice from shaking. "It doesn't make any sense."

"We'd better go look."

Hand in hand they tiptoed up the stairs, jumping at the slightest noise. They examined the floor of each guest room and checked all the bathrooms, feeling around on the tile floors for any sign of moisture but found none. The sinks and tubs were all dry too. The last place they checked was the floor above the wet parlor wall but couldn't come up with any explanation for the leak.

Ellie led the way back down to the parlor with Fran at her heels, neither of them able to understand the flow of water that trickled down the wall. At the bottom of the steps, she turned to take another look at the spot on the ceiling to make sure they had checked exactly the right place on the floor above it. She inhaled with a sharp gasp followed by a shriek from Fran.

The parlor wall was completely dry. No water stain on the ceiling. No dripping.

Despite Fran's warning not to touch it, Ellie went over to the wall that had been soaked less than a half hour earlier. Everything felt dry. Even the faint dust web in the corner that she'd been meaning to whisk away had returned.

"I don't know what's going on here, but the sooner we get that woman's picture put away the better." Fran crept back into the parlor on slow quiet feet as if she were trying to sneak up on Sally unnoticed.

"All right." Shaking off a creepy déjà vu feeling, Ellie climbed up onto the same dining room chair she used the night she came home to find the portrait upside down. With tentative hands she reached for the painting, relieved to see no blood dripping from the edge of the frame this time. Fran helped her rest it on the chair cushion while Ellie stepped down to the floor. Together they carried it out of the parlor, having had to set it down a few times to rest their arms before picking it up again. Finally, they made it to the back hallway.

The door to the storage area was closed.

"That door was open with the light on inside before we went upstairs, wasn't it?" Fran asked with a slight quiver to her voice. "Let's set this down a minute."

With the portrait resting against the wall at her feet, Ellie opened the door and pulled it toward her, only to have the knob fly out of her hand. The door slammed shut with a loud bang.

Unable to move, the two women watched the key turn on its own, clicking the lock into place.

4

Fran fell back against the wall and started to slide. She couldn't seem to catch her breath.

Ellie caught her elbow and guided her into the kitchen where she collapsed into the nearest chair. "Easy, Fran. Take some deep breaths and try to calm down." She pulled a cotton towel from the drawer and ran cold water on it. "Here. Wipe your forehead and the back of your neck with this. You'll feel better."

"This is really scary, Ellie. You've got to get out of here." Fran took the towel but just held it in her lap.

"Why? We're not hurt, are we?"

"Well, no...but..."

"I think this is Sally's way of telling us she doesn't want her picture put away."

"So we just say 'Okay, Sally, no problem' and hang her back up?"

"That wasn't what I meant. I guess I just need to think about this."

"Why don't you do your thinking over at my place? I'm not leaving you alone here with this kind of thing going on."

"I'm not afraid, Fran. Really. Nothing's going to happen to me." Her friend meant well, but Ellie wasn't about to be driven away by the spirits inhabiting her house. Not as long as they were relatively harmless.

Fran stared at her.

"Okay, I'll admit it's a little unnerving, but this is my home. And one way or another, I'm going to work these things out." The conviction in her own voice surprised her. "Now, here's what we'll do. You go home and get a good night's sleep."

Fran rolled her eyes at that but didn't interrupt.

"Sally's portrait will stay right where it is until morning. I'll call Wade back tomorrow, tell him he can get a good look at her before he carries her up to the third floor for me, and either hangs the flower arrangement or brings a different painting from the attic to hang over the fireplace."

"Why not ask your handyman to do that?"

"Fred's great at yard work and furnace repair, but I don't dare trust him with fragile antiques."

Fran still looked skeptical.

"You said yourself that I'll have to deal with Wade's phone call one way or another." Ellie said.

"At least promise you'll lock the front door behind me, go straight back to your apartment, lock that door and stay there until morning."

"I promise."

With reluctance and uncertainty written all over her face, Fran gave her a hug and went out to her car. She opened the window to warn Ellie one more time. "Be careful!"

Ellie locked up behind her friend, then reconsidered the rest of her promise when confronted by the empty wine glasses on her way through the kitchen. She pictured Aunt Carolyn fingering the etched pattern, saying that these glasses would be kept for personal use only and would never go in the dishwasher.

Exhausted from the events of the evening, Ellie yawned and regretted finishing that big bottle, even though it was her favorite wine. It would only take a minute to get the glasses washed and put away, then she'd go straight to bed.

She squirted a drop of dish soap into each glass, pulled a clean cloth from the drawer and turned on the tap. When she pushed her hand inside the glass it split open, the razor sharp edge slicing her finger apart before she realized what had happened. The water in the sink ran red.

Wrapping a kitchen towel around her entire hand with quick movements, Ellie swore under her breath. What a stupid thing to do. She hurried into her apartment holding her arm straight up above her head. With her other hand, she took her medical bag from the closet and carried it into her bathroom. On automatic pilot, she set out bandages, gauze, and tape. As painful as it was, she inspected the inside of the cut to make sure no slivers of glass remained in the wound. No stitches needed, she decided. Butterfly bandages would hold it together well enough.

It was tougher than she anticipated with only one usable hand. By the time she got the bleeding stopped and put the last bandage on her finger to protect it, she was starting to feel light headed. Her watery knees held up long enough for her to take some pain killers to fight the intense throbbing, rinse the blood out of the sink and change into her nightgown.

Her injured hand rested on top of the covers as she sank into deep sleep. In a foggy dream, her hand started to move on its own, rise up and back down again. Then she felt the bandage loosen. Large hands around her own. Muffled noises. As hard as she tried to pull her eyelids open, she couldn't force herself to wake up to see what was happening. A soft soothing voice murmured to her in gentle tones, using words she couldn't make out at first. Then the words became clearer.

Ellen. Please allow me to take care of this for you.

She stopped struggling to wake up. It didn't seem necessary now. The voice was familiar to her. Her mouth moved but nothing came out. How she wanted to talk to him. The spirit of the kind doctor who needed her to tend the wounds of his men was now tending her own.

"Yes," she said to him in a dreamlike voice. "Take care of me as I will take care of you. I want to help heal your heart, the torture in your soul that keeps you here."

Indeed, we have much to give one another. Rest now.

The next morning, Ellie lay in the same position she was in when she fell asleep, except her hand was underneath the covers, which had been tucked neatly under her chin. Waking up was a slow process. It was a struggle to raise her eyelids, even just a little. Through narrow slits she could make out a mix of white and blue through the window. She'd never even closed the blinds last night.

She felt some slight tenderness when she moved her hand beneath the covers, but much less than she expected. With a houseful of guests arriving, she couldn't let a sore finger get in her way.

Hoping her cut hadn't bled during the night, she tried to pull her arms out from under to the covers to take a look, but she seemed to be wrapped in a soft cocoon. Eventually she pulled all the covers off and sat up.

Ellie stared down at the injured hand in her lap. Instead of the butterfly bandages she'd placed over the cut last night, a piece of faded fabric was wound around her finger. The edges were torn and tied in a neat knot. She was sure this dressing came from the roll of muslin bandage that she'd held in her hand last night from the box of Dr. Alexander's surgical instruments.

Under the bright light in the bathroom, she slowly worked the knot loose and untied the bandage. The cut had been sewn together with the soft silken thread from the spool in his medical kit.

She touched it with her other hand, remembering the dream. It wasn't a dream though. It had been real. The gentle words he'd spoken came back to her. Her initial awe and wonder melted into warmth and tenderness. How could she be attracted to a man who didn't exist?

But Dr. Grant Alexander really did exist. The bandage on her finger was solid proof.

Ellie sat back down on her bed, unable to take her eyes off the stitches in her finger. A quick glance at the clock told her a half hour had passed in what seemed like less than a minute. Time to get rolling.

Unfortunately, spending her entire day trying to communicate with Dr. Alexander wouldn't be possible, considering all that needed to be done. She hoped the portrait was still in the back hallway where she and Fran had left it.

She got up, brewed a pot of strong coffee, showered and dressed before calling Wade, rehearsing in her mind what she intended to say. He answered immediately and said he'd be right over. It was the shortest phone conversation Ellie ever had with anyone.

Knowing Wade would soon be on her doorstep gave her the courage to face the back hallway where she and Fran had abandoned the portrait. She kicked herself for not making sure the portrait was okay before she called him. He'd be more than upset with her if anything had happened to it. She was relieved to find it exactly as it was last night.

Searching the face of the woman in front of her, Ellie was beginning to wonder if Wade's feelings about Sally were mutual. Maybe if she treated Wade better, Sally wouldn't be so angry. On the other hand, it might make Sally jealous and Ellie didn't want that either. One way to find out, she supposed.

Ellie noticed that Sally's expression appeared somewhat smug this morning. Maybe her imagination was getting the best of her. How could the expression on a face in a painting change the way this one does? There was only one explanation. Sally's spirit still dwelled here and it was strong enough to alter her portrait. Not enough for the average person to notice, but Ellie could see it. Now that she thought about it, her guests never mentioned anything much. Just an occasional comment about the beauty of the woman in the painting.

Absorbed in speculation about the mystery surrounding Sally and her portrait, Ellie jumped when the doorbell chimed. Had she not been expecting him, she never would have recognized the man who stood before her. Previously pale, his swollen face was bright red. He reached up with a puffy inflamed hand and pulled the baseball cap from his head. His lifeless straight hair had been scorched, revealing irregular stubbles sprouting from a blotchy scalp. He looked terrible.

"Ellie," he mumbled with a short nod.

She held the door open for him, discreetly keeping her injured hand out of sight as much as possible.

Wade stepped inside and placed a package in the corner without mentioning it.

Ellie barely noticed. She was still recovering from the shock of his appearance. He seemed to have aged at least ten years. "Goodness," she couldn't help saying, "Are you all right? What happened?" No point in letting on that she'd heard about the fire from Fran a while back. She didn't expect him to still look so bad from the explosion after all this time.

"A slight accident," Wade said. "Not like a big explosion or a fire or anything."

"Then what?"

"I'm working on a big project, okay? It just isn't turning out the way I'd hoped." Then he saw at the empty spot above the fireplace and turned back to Ellie and shouted, "What have you done with her?"

"Sit down for a minute. Please."

"No. First tell me where you put Sally's portrait. I need to see it."

She didn't expect him to be so upset just because she had moved it. How was she going to explain having the portrait in the hall without admitting that she'd planned to lock it away, so he couldn't steal it?

"I moved it."

"Why?"

"I ... ah ... I'm going to have the parlor repainted. After all the guests coming through here over the summer, I realized the walls were showing some wear and there's some dirt that didn't come off with regular cleaning."

"The parlor must be wallpapered, not painted."

"Pardon me?"

"I have an old tintype that will give you an idea of the pattern you need to find. You'll find it quite tasteful. Much better than this beige paint. More authentic. True to the house." His looked back at the empty spot above the fireplace. "True to Sally," he whispered.

The nurse inside Ellie couldn't ignore his burns. "Your hands," she said.

"What about them?"

"They're so red. They must be painful."

"Speaking of hands, what happened to yours?"

"Oh, it's nothing. I just broke a glass last night. It doesn't hurt. Look, I'll get my medical kit from the bedroom. I have some cream will help soothe those burns."

"Wait a minute. How do you know they're burns?"

"I'm a nurse, remember?"

With a strong clear voice, Dr. Alexander interrupted the thoughts inside her head. *Make an ointment. Use bark from the sweet elder tree out back. Boil it, then strain it. Mix the liquid with honey and spread it on the skin.*

Wade started to protest again, but he stopped in mid-sentence when he saw the stunned expression on Ellie's face. "What's the matter?"

So, he hadn't heard the voice. "We'd better sit down for a minute," she said. "I have something to tell you."

Wade studied her face with a soft look in his eyes, one she'd never seen before. "Yes. Okay. I have something to tell you too." Suddenly, seeing Sally's portrait wasn't quite so urgent.

Wade perched himself on the edge of the sofa in the parlor, leaning toward the overstuffed chair where Ellie sat with her legs folded beneath her.

This was a college professor she was talking to, one with extensive historical and scientific knowledge. She wanted him to take what she was about to say seriously without becoming impatient, so she chose her words carefully.

"I believe the inn is inhabited by two spirits. Both have communicated with me."

Wade jumped to his feet. "You've talked with Sally? What did she say?"

"Sit down." No need to get testy with him, she thought, and added a "Please" before continuing. "I didn't exactly talk with her. I didn't have to. Sally makes her desires quite clear without conversation."

Once he sat down again, Ellie told Wade what happened after he dropped her off the night they had dinner and everything that happened since then, even though he kept interrupting her with more questions.

She was more interested in what he knew about Dr. Alexander, but he kept bringing the conversation back to Sally. For a while, it seemed like they were just talking in circles. After Wade was satisfied there was nothing more Ellie could tell him, he was ready to share what he knew about the doctor. It wasn't much.

"From her letters, I know that Sally was fond of him. I think she hoped he'd marry her and take her back to Boston where he lived before the war. Becoming a doctor's wife must have seemed like a life of leisure to her compared to running this place on her own."

"I assumed that if he had married her, you would have mentioned it the night we had dinner. You didn't mention him that night at all."

"Because he hurt Sally!" he shouted, jumping off the sofa and waving his arms. "Why would I want to even think about a man who rejected her affection and rode out of her life as if she didn't matter?"

"Don't get so worked up. I'm just trying to understand what's going on in my own home here. Okay?"

"Sorry." He sat down again. "Look, from what I know about him, Grant Alexander was a good doctor. The wounded men who were treated here told their families he was the most compassionate doctor they knew. My great-great-great grandmother, Martha Savage, spent a lot of time here trying to help Sally. She wrote letters home for the wounded men who couldn't write their own. In her diary, she wrote that the doctor rarely slept. Stayed rail thin because he gave his rations to the men he was trying to heal. Said they needed it more than he did."

"So, the only thing you have against this man is the fact that he didn't marry Sally?"

"Isn't that enough?"

She assumed that to be a rhetorical question and didn't answer. Instead, she suggested he take a close look at her finger and then told him about the dream that wasn't really a dream.

He seemed impressed, but not as blown away by it as she expected. Ellie was a little disappointed in his reaction. He acted like he thought the doctor did nice work, but this sort of thing happened every day.

Should she get the cream from her medical bag or follow Dr. Alexander's instructions? She'd seen a few patients who had put honey or butter on their burns before coming to the ER but didn't see them for follow up care and she certainly knew nothing about mixing it with sweet elder. In fact, she'd never heard of sweet elder. Maybe it would work just as well as her modern cream. One way to find out.

"A few minutes ago, Dr. Alexander gave me a remedy to try on your skin."

"His voice told you this? He gave you a remedy for me?"

"The voice of his spirit. I'm sure of it." She repeated what Dr. Alexander had told her.

"So he knows I'm here. Amazing."

"Tell you what," she suggested. "If you're sure your hands can manage it, we'll move the portrait from the hallway and lay it on the dining room table. Take all the time you need with it while I cut the elder bark and make the ointment. Deal?"

"Okay."

Minutes later, she was standing at the stove, boiling, stirring, and straining while Wade leaned over the table inspecting every detail of Sally's face. Sometimes he stood back to admire her from across the room and sometimes he moved in close. Every now and then she'd hear him talking to Sally under his breath. At first, she thought it was weird but then decided it probably wasn't much different from the conversation she'd had with the spirit of Dr. Alexander yesterday. This rationalization made her feel uneasy, as if she'd somehow crossed a line and was heading down a path that would alter her life forever.

Wade stood up straight and cleared his throat. "Thank you," he said, turning to Ellie. "I won't be taking her with me after all. This is her house. It's where she belongs."

Ellie put the cooled elder bark ointment in a glass jar for Wade, then together they carried Sally's portrait to the parlor and put it back above the fireplace. It truly was the centerpiece of the room and Ellie could see how much he loved it.

Wade went over to the corner where he'd left the package when he came in, picked it up and unwrapped it.

Ellie gasped when he handed her the small framed painting. It was a lovely oil replica of the front of the inn, with a huge lilac bush in full bloom at the front corner of the house.

"Where did you get this?" she asked in a whisper.

He shuffled his feet, suddenly at a loss for words for a moment. "Had it for years. Let's say I came to acquire it during one of the darker stretches of my life. Paid dearly for it. Not in terms of cash but ... well, let's just say those days are over now. I want you to have it."

"Oh, it's beautiful." She hugged it against her. "Don't you see, Wade? This proves it's his voice. He told me where to plant the lilac. He said it belonged out front."

He came closer and put his hand lightly on her shoulder. "I believe you. I believe everything."

Ellie hugged him gently and brushed her lips against his cheek, surprised that his reassurance mattered so much to her. She wasn't the least bit attracted to Wade, but their connection with the spirits from the past brought them close in an odd sort of way. He'd come a long way from the jerk he was when they first met.

"Earlier you said you had something you wanted to tell me. What was it?" Ellie asked.

He licked his lips and looked at her intently. "Ellie, do you believe time travel is possible?"

5

llie made her usual quality check of the inn from top to bottom to be sure everything was ready for the guests that would soon arrive. There was just enough time to pick some of the few remaining fresh flowers from the yard. She arranged them in a crystal vase on the dining room table, adding a light fragrance and a touch of hominess to the room.

Better to stay busy and set aside her conversations with Wade for now, she thought, but it wasn't so easy. His ideas about going back in time to be with Sally were exciting but at the same time dangerous and foolhardy. No wonder he was often covered with burns, considering the ridiculous experiments he was conducting. Nothing Wade said surprised or upset her anymore. Maybe because his feelings for Sally were identical to her own feelings for Grant Alexander. If Wade were successful at time travel, and he gave her the opportunity to live with Grant in 1863, would she go?

She wasn't sure but didn't have the luxury of mulling the idea over any longer.

Satisfied that every detail had been tended to, she poured a tall glass of cold lemonade and carried it over to the desktop computer. The reservation software system brought up the list of guests, their contact information, and the dates they had reserved.

Among them was the name she was hoping to find: Dr. Harold Lyster, the retired doctor from Chicago who often stayed at Ivy Garden when he was in the area working on a project related to Civil War medicine. He planned to be here on the first of October.

Ellie sometimes wondered if he had been attracted to Aunt Carolyn. His wife died several years ago. Something about the way he and Aunt Carolyn had gazed at each other when they thought Ellie wasn't looking that made her curious, but she never asked.

She knew he was familiar with most of the antique dealers and restoration craftsmen in the area. He could recommend the best place to have the instruments cleaned and framed by someone who would know the proper way to display them.

When she heard footsteps on the porch, she assumed her guests were starting to arrive until she heard Myra Keller calling her familiar "Yoo Hoo!"

"Come on in, Myra. I was just doing some paperwork at the desk."

"I brought you some fresh oatmeal cookies!" Her cheery tone turned dismal when her attention turned to the picture above the fireplace. "Oh, dear," she moaned and walked toward it.

"What's wrong?"

"Sally's picture. It looks different somehow. What did you do?"

Still shaking her head, she crossed the room and planted her feet close to Ellie's. Too close. "That professor was here again. I saw him. Did you let him move her or something?"

How could she tell this woman to mind her own business without being rude? Her breath came out in a huff. "Actually, I was thinking of wallpapering the parlor over the winter and I took it down for a short time. Myra, there's no reason I can't rearrange things here occasionally, is there?"

"Yes. There sure is. Let me tell you something. Now, I know your Aunt Carolyn had no trouble with…" She glanced around and lowered her voice as if someone might overhear her. "Spirits," she whispered.

"We're alone, Myra. You don't have to whisper."

"Yes, I do." She continued her story in a hushed voice. "See, that picture of Sally has been in that exact spot over the fireplace since the days when she lived here. Your friend, Mr. Savage, he could tell you that. The people who owned the place before your aunt bought it, they tried to move it once.

Over to our house all the time they were, telling George and me about the strange things that happened here because of it. Things moving around on their own. Peculiar noises. Voices. Once they hung Sally up there over the fireplace where she belonged, everything was normal again. What I'm saying is, don't mess with her. Do you get my meaning?"

"I understand." Ellie hoped that by not arguing, Myra would consider the subject closed and go back home. No such luck.

"Now don't go changing things around. I'm telling you, she gets mad."

"There's nothing to worry about here really. Everything's fine." Walking toward the door to hold it open for Myra, she added, "My guests will be arriving any minute and I have a few last-minute things to attend to. Thanks for the cookies."

"All right, then. But if you need anything, you be sure to come right over."

Ellie closed the door and moved the plate of cookies from the coffee table to the kitchen. Myra was a good baker, but Ellie always made sure that anything served to her guests came from Martha and only Martha. She set out a pitcher of lemonade, another of iced tea and some glasses while she thought about her neighbor's visit. Myra had just proved that Ellie wasn't the only one who noticed the changes in Sally's face.

Later that evening, she sat down in her apartment and held painting of the inn that Wade had given her. She noticed the subtle changes in the colors depending on the angle of the light and admired the painstaking detail. She just couldn't get enough of it.

Then she noticed something she was sure hadn't been there before. The shadow of a man in uniform standing near the house. An officer with wavy gray hair and a heavy gray beard. Through his body, she could see the leaves on the lilac bush behind him.

Then he was gone.

September sped by, each day a flurry of activity getting new arrivals settled, making restaurant recommendations for dinner, answering questions about the house, and making notes about the restoration work and third floor remodeling that she planned to do over the winter.

On October first when she was about ready to go back to her apartment to relax for the first time since she got up that morning, Harold Lyster walked in the front door, brushing his hand across what appeared to be a soup stain in the center of his white shirt. A creature of habit, he always went to dinner early. Eating too late in the evening gave him indigestion, he said.

"Ellie!" he said, walking toward her with his hands outstretched. "I want to say again how sorry I am about your Aunt Carolyn. We didn't have much opportunity to talk earlier with everyone arriving at once." He took both of her hands in his and looked into her face. "Such a shock. Are you managing all right?"

"I miss her, as you can well imagine. We were very close."

"I know."

His soft sympathetic tone released a flow of unexpected tears that spilled from her eyes before she could catch them. She brushed them away with the back of her hand and pulled a tissue from her pocket. What a fine physician he must have been. Such a kind and gentle man. When he reached out to touch her arm, she allowed him to give her a soft hug before they sat down to talk.

After they were interrupted a second time by guests milling about, Ellie suggested they go back to the sitting room in her apartment. They made themselves comfortable on opposite sides of her sofa, and he noticed the painting she'd left on the end table.

"I really like that picture you have there, Ellie. It must have been painted before the troops came through here."

"I think so. The signature of the artist is hard to read but the date is clear. May 1863. Lilacs always bloom in May." Feeling the need to explain why it was simply sitting on the end table, she added, "I keep meaning to hang it on the wall, but when I hold it in my hands, sometimes what I see in the painting changes. The colors, I mean."

"Is the painting what motivated you to plant the lilac in the corner there?"

Ellie took a deep breath, considering whether it was wise to tell Harold about Dr. Alexander. She hesitated long enough for him to know she was holding something back.

"What is it, Ellie?"

When she told him about the instruments she'd found in the attic, how she felt drawn to them, the things that Dr. Alexander had said, and about the electricity in the air when she heard the voice, he didn't seem surprised at any of it.

"I've known for years about the spirits in this house. Your aunt brushed it all off as local lore kept alive only to attract the tourists. What you and I have experienced with Dr. Alexander is something entirely different."

Ellie sat up straight, knocking the throw pillow she'd been resting against over the arm of the sofa and onto the floor. "You've heard his voice, too?"

"No, I haven't heard Dr. Alexander's voice, but I know when he's around."

She couldn't believe it. "You never mentioned it."

"For the same reason you didn't. Not everyone has the same attitude about these things. Hollywood has convinced most people that spirits are out to do us harm, that they're something to be feared. I know that's not true, because my dear wife speaks to me from the other side now and then."

Ellie smiled. She should have known.

"There are very few people I could talk to about that and now you're one of them. Talk of ghosts tends to scare most folks. But I believe they're no different from the people they were when they were alive. Good ones and bad ones everywhere. Many want to be near those they loved during their time on earth. Some are just trying to take care of their unfinished business before they can move on to the afterlife. Well, that's how I look at it, anyway."

Suddenly, Ellie wanted to tell him everything. "When these things started to happen, especially with the pearls, I thought it was Aunt Carolyn. As much as I would love to communicate with her, it's become clear that the spirit I'm hearing from is Dr. Alexander."

"Oh, he's very much alive here. Or thinks he is. He's still waiting for more wounded to arrive. His job is to ease their misery and heal them. That's what's holding him here. Until he's satisfied that the last man has been cared for, he simply can't leave."

"Do you think there's a way to help him move on? That's what he's supposed to do, isn't it?"

"Eventually, yes, but my guess is he'll go when he's ready. Not before."

"Have you actually seen him?"

"No, not even in the mirror like you have. But there have been other signs. Often when I was working on my manuscripts late at night, I'd come downstairs for a cup of tea and a snack. Back at the desk, I'd find my medical journals had been moved while I was gone. Pages turned from where I'd left off. The two books of mine in the library would be moved off the shelf and I'd find them open on the table in there. Things like that. I guess that's why I believe it's the spirit of the doctor. Who else would be interested in those things?" He paused for a moment, then shook his head and added, "No, there isn't any other way to explain it."

Ellie sank back against the cushions, needing some time to take this in. They sat quietly, listening to the sounds coming from other parts of the house. A few more guests returned from dinner. Two of them announced they'd sit in the wicker chairs out on the front porch for a while. Another climbed the stairs to his room and exchanged pleasantries with one coming down.

"I'd like to show you something," Ellie said and brought out the wooden box from the floor of her closet. She never tired of looking through the medical instruments inside, and as she expected, Harold shared her enthusiasm.

"This is unbelievable. Those are his initials on the lid. G.F.A."

"I know. He told me."

Harold looked up at her with a tender smile. "He told you. Truly amazing."

"I was thinking of having them refurbished in some way and maybe displaying them in the parlor." She braced herself for his reaction. Half of her was hoping he'd say he knew just the right restoration specialist who could do it, and the other half was afraid he'd say they belong to history and should be donated to the park service or the historical society.

To her relief, Harold was excited. "Excellent idea! Excellent. Tomorrow we can drive over to Gettysburg. I know of a good antiques man over there who will treat them with care and breathe life back into them."

"I believe Dr. Alexander has already brought them back to life. I can feel a crackle of energy whenever I open the box."

"I felt it too. Shall we plan to go after breakfast?"

"I'll be ready."

They walked out to the parlor together where Ellie said goodnight to him. The last of Martha's cookies on the cut glass plate begged to be eaten, so Ellie complied while putting away the lemonade and iced tea and loading the glasses in the dishwasher. As winter approached, the ritual would transition to teas, hot chocolate, and spiced cider.

Just as she was finishing up, one of Ellie's first-time guests, a young woman, came downstairs and asked permission to play the piano.

"I don't know that I've ever heard it played. It probably needs tuning, but you're welcome to give it a try. No later than nine o'clock though, please."

With a soft thank you, the woman sat down on the bench and began to play a tender sweet tune. Ellie drifted over to her favorite chair, sat down, and put her feet up. Leaning back with her eyes closed, she imagined the house as it was years ago when Sally and her husband had finished building it. All the hopes and dreams they must have shared. Wade had told her they put this grand piano in the parlor after the floor was finished and then built the walls of the house around it. In the early years of their marriage, they often entertained friends in this room. It must have been beautiful. Until the war invaded their home and the top of the piano became an operating table.

The tune changed abruptly to discordant repetition of two or three keys, then stopped completely.

"I'm sorry," the woman said. "I don't know what happened."

"Something must be stuck," Ellie responded, opening her eyes. She thought there was a flutter of movement around Sally's portrait but when she looked closer, it was gone.

The woman tried the same tune an octave higher, then an octave lower but the keys remained silent. "I'm sorry. I hope I didn't break your piano."

"Please don't worry," Ellie assured her and glanced back up at Sally's face. "I'm sure you didn't hurt anything." In fact, she was quite positive it was nothing this woman had done that put a stop to the music.

"Why don't you try it again in the morning? Sometimes temperature and humidity can affect things."

Appearing relieved to have avoided any blame, the woman said good night and went upstairs.

Ellie waited a few minutes, and then tried several of the keys herself with the same result. She tried lifting up the top of the piano to look inside but couldn't hold it up long enough to prop it open. Her curiosity got the best of her and she climbed the stairs to Harold's room. She tapped on his door and waited for what seemed like several minutes but probably wasn't.

He opened the door and stood aside to let her in. He took off his glasses and rubbed his eyes before he even looked at her. As she expected, the desk in his room was covered with books and papers.

"Sorry to interrupt, but I wondered if you could come downstairs to give me a hand with the piano. One of the other guests just tried to play it and..."

"Yes, I heard. Lovely tune. Too bad she stopped so soon."

"That's just it. She kept on playing but the sound simply stopped."

"Let's have a look."

Together they went downstairs and tested the keys again. Still nothing. They lifted the top of the piano, propped it open, and looked inside. The long tops of the keys beneath the lid were oozing a thick substance that glistened in the dim light. It was wet, sticky and red.

A long moan echoed from deep inside the piano. The first was followed by others, becoming a chorus of terrible cries that made them both back away. They looked at each other and back to the piano in horror but neither knew how make the screaming stop.

When the noise finally faded, the blood on the tops of the keys beneath the lid started to dry up and then it disappeared. All was quiet again as if nothing had happened.

The horrible screams continued inside Ellie's head and she couldn't shake the chill they gave her. Pulling her sweater tightly around her, she rubbed her arms and stared at the open piano. In all her years of working in the Emergency Room, she'd never heard anything even close to this.

"Are you all right, Ellie? Your face is a ghastly shade of white."

Her voice trembled when she responded. "I think so. It's just so..."

"Come here." Harold held out his arms.

Ellie allowed herself to be comforted in Harold's embrace and rested her head on his shoulder. He had a fatherly way about him and she was not embarrassed by the way he treated her as if she were his daughter.

Finally, her gasps slowed, and she was able to take a deep breath. It helped. When she lifted her head to look at him, she said, "You're a bit on the pale side yourself."

"I'm not surprised," Harold admitted. "It all happened so suddenly. The chill...the awful chill that came over me when that screaming started. I've never heard anything like that in all my life. The whole room sounded like it was filled with dying men, every one of them in excruciating pain." He shook his head as if to cast off the eerie feeling the experience brought to both of them. "I won't forget this as long as I live."

"Neither will I," she said looking into his face.

Harold returned her long solemn stare, a new bond forged between them now, after having shared a few moments of what it must have been like in this house after the battle. He helped her close the piano and cover the keys.

For a few minutes they didn't say anything. It had been so easy for her to say she lived in a Civil War home that had been used as a hospital after the nearby battle. Tonight, the true implications of those words sank in and she would never again allow herself to utter them lightly.

"I wonder why no one came running down the stairs when that happened," Ellie said.

"If I had to guess, I'd say we were the only ones who heard it. It's a good thing you came upstairs to get me." Having regained his composure, he held her by the shoulders and said, "Now let's go back to your apartment and I'll make you a cup of hot tea with a splash of whiskey. It'll help calm your nerves so you can sleep."

Ellie only drank tea when she didn't feel well, which wasn't often. Harold must have known that hot tea was exactly what she needed. It sounded good to her right now. She waited on the sofa and soon he brought a tray from the kitchen with a steaming teapot and two cups. "Here we are," he announced. "Just what the doctor ordered."

The first sip tasted sweet and hot with just enough whiskey to warm her all over. "Thanks, Harold," she said. "You ought to come to stay here more often."

He filled a cup for himself, took it over to the armchair and sat down to face her. "To tell you the truth, I'd like to. It's just that it's not the same here without Carolyn. I keep expecting to see her bustling around the corner of the dining room, humming to herself."

Ellie nodded. "I know what you mean."

"Don't get me wrong, now. You're doing a fine job here. Excellent job. It's just different now, that's all."

"Different for both of us."

They sat sipping their tea in silence a little while longer. Ellie felt her eyelids getting heavy and leaned her head against the back of the sofa.

"I'll leave you alone now, if you'll promise to go right to bed."

"I can't think of doing anything else."

"Good. Call if you need me."

"You're not planning to do any more work on your book tonight, are you? I mean after all that just happened?"

"I just experienced the chaos of a Civil War hospital with my own ears. What better time to write about it?"

"I suppose so." The man was amazing. "Good night then."

"Try to sleep now. Good night."

Ellie waited until she heard his door close on the floor above. Then she went out to the parlor, lit a candle and sat in her favorite chair for a while. The cold eerie feeling was replaced by a calm awareness that, for a short while, the past had become the present here in this house. Maybe a thin veil was really all that separated us from a different time and place.

Alone in the darkness except for the candle, she waited, hoping Grant would visit her. When nothing happened, she walked over to the mirror and peered into the glass, not looking at her reflection, but past it for something more.

Then the white wave of mist she'd been hoping for appeared. Faint at first, then stronger. A glow of happiness spread through her as she watched the mist crystallize into

Grant's handsome face. Her heart fluttered like a schoolgirl's when he looked at her.

Ellen. Don't let Sally upset you.

"What happened tonight was Sally's doing?"

Yes.

"I thought so. Her piano hasn't been played since the battle, has it?"

Sally won't allow anyone to play it.

"Why not?"

The music brings memories of the way her life used to be before the war. She is filled with resentment because of what has happened to her home. The piano is my operating table, you know.

"Then it was the blood of your men that I saw tonight?"

Yes. Blood of the men I couldn't save.

"But you tried to save them, Grant. You did everything you could."

The white mist burst from the mirror and swirled around her, blanketing her in warmth of an intensity she'd never known. She reached out and put her fingers into the mist. Another hand touched hers. It grasped her fingers in a gentle but invisible caress. Lips kissed the back of her hand and the gesture melted her heart.

Thank you, Ellen. I know you understand.

6

Previous encounters with the spirit of Grant Alexander had left Ellie awestruck and bewildered. Not this time. Tonight, he had reached out to her, igniting a flame that would glow in her heart forever. Ellen was no longer just the name he called her. When she was with him, she felt herself becoming Ellen, an entirely different woman from the Ellie she'd been all her life and the thought of it thrilled her. She wanted more and waited in front of the mirror clinging to the last wisp of his presence, unwilling to let go of him.

When the alarm clock went off the next morning, she couldn't believe it was time to get up already. She thought she had just closed her eyes for a minute. Her first attempt at standing up brought a weird feeling of weakness. Not unpleasant, just odd.

Thoughts of last night preoccupied her mind as she followed her normal morning routine. After rinsing out the mound of shampoo that had cascaded in her eyes, she caught herself squeezing liniment onto her toothbrush instead of toothpaste. She threw the toothbrush in the trash and sliced a paper cut into her thumb when she took a new one out of its cardboard packaging. If the hot shower didn't help, maybe a cup of strong coffee would.

It didn't. In the kitchen while helping prepare breakfast for the guests, she burned the first batch of pancakes. Martha convinced her to see to things out in the dining room and let her take over the kitchen. After all, she was hired to be the cook, wasn't she? Ellie had to remind herself again that it was important to allow her employees to do their jobs instead of always trying to help them. Another aspect of innkeeping that she had trouble learning. As a nurse in the Emergency Room, she'd been accustomed to diving into whatever needed to be done. It was obvious today that her staff could manage much better without her assistance.

After breakfast, Harold lingered in the dining room after the others went on their way. Concerned about the day's cloudy start, most were anxious to get started with their activities early to avoid getting soaked later.

"I'm ready whenever you are," Harold said. "No rush."

"Just give me a few minutes to finish up here."

Ten minutes later, Ellie stood in the doorway, the box of instruments cradled in her arms. She'd wrapped it in a large bath towel and placed it in a heavy plastic bag to protect it. Had it been a treasure chest filled with gold, she couldn't have handled it with greater care.

Once settled in the front seat, she was ready to tell Harold about last night. "Did you happen to hear anything last evening after we closed up the piano?"

"Not that I recollect, no. I thought you had gone to bed and as you know, once I get buried in my work, not much disturbs me. Why?"

After Ellie told him about Grant's visit last night, Harold said, "I would have come back downstairs had I known."

"It's all right. In fact, it's better that you didn't. The slightest interruption seems to make Dr. Alexander disappear. Even a normal sound, like the phone ringing. Who knows? If you'd come back, nothing may have happened."

"Well, it certainly seems as though the good doctor has developed an attraction to you, Ellie."

"I hope so."

"The feeling is mutual, isn't it? I can see it on your face."

She smiled as he pulled over to the curb.

In all her antique hunts with Aunt Carolyn, Ellie had never been inside this particular shop. She didn't know how they'd missed it. Every aisle was filled with beautiful pieces ranging from jewelry to massive furniture, most of it in excellent condition. Judging from the quality of his goods, the owner of the shop seemed worthy of the task he was about to undertake.

"I wonder if we might speak to you about some potential restoration work?" Ellie asked the shopkeeper.

The man eyed the box in her arms with undisguised curiosity. "Of course. Please come to the back of the shop."

Ellie placed her bundle on a table, unwrapped it, and opened the lid. As she and Harold had expected, the shopkeeper was impressed with the condition of the instruments and eager to restore them. He held the pieces up one at a time and examined everything thoroughly.

"Ah, this is quite a rare find. Where did you get it?"

She and Harold exchanged glances. Best policy was always to tell the truth. "Buried in my attic," Ellie said. "Literally."

"Splendid! Do you plan to sell it? If so, I would be very interested."

"No, that's not why I brought it."

"Too bad. It would make a fine addition to my own personal collection."

"It's not for sale," Ellie repeated, just to make sure he understood. "I'm interested in having the box and all its contents restored to their original condition."

"I was telling Ms. Michaels here about your splendid reputation for restoration work," added Harold. "Perhaps you could show us a few pieces you've done?"

The shopkeeper led them to a set of shelves at the side of the room and presented a box like Ellie's, but smaller and in excellent condition. He opened the lid revealing a gleaming set of polished silverware. "When this was brought to me last month, you wouldn't have recognized it as the same box you see now." He showed her the before and after photos he'd taken of it.

If her box of instruments looked as good as this when he'd finished, Ellie felt confident she'd be satisfied with his work. After he showed her the dressing table he was working on in the corner of the room, she was convinced. The table was half finished. Here she could see the way it looked when he started on one side and the result of his work on the other.

"How long do you think it will take to bring my box and all its contents back to their original condition?"

"A few weeks, a month perhaps. Would that be acceptable to you?"

"As long as you do as good a job with this as you have with the other items you showed me, yes."

When the time came to go, she realized she was about to leave behind this precious connection to the spirit that dwelled in her home. Suddenly it didn't matter how well this man restored antiques, he couldn't possibly be worthy of the task. No one was.

"I've changed my mind," she told Harold. Her voice quivered. "I can't do it." She ran her hand over the top of the box and held it close. "I just can't leave it."

Both men peered at her, then at each other.

She saw Harold give the shopkeeper a slight nod and gesture toward the front of the shop, a signal that it was time to busy himself elsewhere for a few minutes out of earshot.

The shopkeeper took the hint.

Harold put his hand on her shoulder and she trembled beneath his touch. He reached out to take the box from her arms and she handed it over to him without a word. Her fingertips drifted away from the lid of the box in a long slow motion as she tried to stretch out the final touch for as long as she could. A troubling heaviness filled her heart. What had she been thinking?

Harold set the box down on the table. "What is it, Ellie?" Harold asked, trying to read her face.

She shook her head and shrugged but couldn't find words to describe the way she felt. If she didn't understand it herself, how could she explain it to Harold?

"This shop is the best in town. You won't find a man with more experience."

"I don't doubt that. We've seen what excellent work he does. It's not that I don't trust him." Ellie took both of Harold's hands in hers and held them. "Maybe this sad feeling I have is Dr. Alexander's way of trying to tell me not to disturb what had been his. I mean, he might need these instruments when his wounded men arrive and won't be able to find them because I've taken them away and didn't tell him where they are."

She moved away from Harold, picked up the box and brought it close one more time, running her hands over it in a soothing motion. Tears welled in the corners of her eyes and she watched one fall to the lid of the box. With her thumb, she wiped it away from the wooden surface and told herself how irrational her behavior was. She had to hope Dr. Alexander would be pleased with the result, Ellie took a deep breath, set the box down, let go of it and stepped away from the table.

The shopkeeper must have run into this sort of emotional attachment before and returned to reassure her. "Ms. Michaels, I promise you this box and its contents will be well cared for. You'll be quite pleased with my work. You'll see," he told her. How she wanted to believe him.

She held onto Harold's arm and leaned against him as they watched the shopkeeper carry the box away and out of sight.

Harold handed her his handkerchief without saying a word.

"Thanks," she said and dried her face with it.

Harold steered her away from the back of the shop and pointed out some of the merchandise displayed for sale. By the time they left, she'd selected a few items to purchase for the inn: some linens, a narrow table for the library and a basket that would look perfect on the hearth. With a little maneuvering, they managed to get everything they bought into the back of the car just as the drizzle became a downpour.

They stopped at a diner on the way back for a bowl of chili. Ellie wasn't hungry but felt obligated to have lunch with Harold in return for his kindness.

"This weather sure did change in a hurry," Harold remarked. "Yesterday I was sweating in the sun during my afternoon walk. Today I can't seem to get warm at all. I guess it's that time of year."

"This front moved in pretty fast. Good thing all my guests are staying again tonight. Not a good day for travel if the prediction of thunderstorms and heavy rain is accurate."

By the time their bowls of chili arrived, the melancholy feeling that Ellie had been grappling with all morning had faded. She was beginning to feel more sociable and was ready to eat now that her appetite was returning.

Their easy conversation flowed from one topic to the next all through lunch and on the way home. When they passed by the Chamber of Commerce on their way through town, Ellie asked Harold to stop so she could pick up a fresh supply of brochures and an updated calendar of town events. By the time they pulled into the driveway, it was mid-afternoon.

Harold suggested they leave the new purchases in the car until the rain stopped, but Ellie insisted on taking the basket inside. With this heavy cloud cover, the sky would be getting dark early tonight and she wanted to light a fire in the parlor fireplace to warm her guests when they returned at the end of their day. The basket was the perfect place for newspapers and kindling.

She hung her wet jacket on the chair in her apartment kitchen. After fluffing the dampness from her hair and refreshing her makeup, she went out to the desk and found four messages on her answering machine.

Fran had called to see how things were going. The muffler had fallen off her car this morning and it was in the shop until tomorrow. She'd be a little short of cash until payday, but if

Ellie wanted to do something together this weekend, maybe go somewhere on Sunday, weather permitting of course, Fran would be interested. Call back when you can.

The second call was a reservation for the end of the month.

Wade called, sounding very excited and also very polite compared to past messages. Would Ellie please call and tell him when it would be convenient for him to drop by?

The last message was the very formal voice of a man identifying himself as Harold Lyster's nephew. "My mother, Harold's sister, suffered a massive stroke this morning and she's not expected to live very long. Please have Harold call me back as soon as possible. I can't get through on his cell phone."

She wrote down the number, ran upstairs and tapped on the open door of his room. "I have a message for you, Harold." When he opened the door she said, "Bad news, I'm afraid."

"What is it?"

"Your sister has had a stroke. Your nephew wants you to call him right away. His message was on the answering machine. Here's the number in case you need it." She handed him the note.

"Oh, no. How bad is it? Did he say?"

"He said that you should call him right away." Ellie thought it best that the details come directly from Harold's nephew rather than from her.

He took the slip of paper from her hand and picked up his cell phone. "I always forget to turn this thing back on when I'm not working."

Ellie lingered in the hallway as he dialed the number, to see if there was anything else she might be able to do for him. A chill came over her as if a cold breeze were blowing in the upstairs hall. The cold wet weather that moved in overnight had crept into every corner of the inn. She turned the dial on the upstairs thermostat until the furnace clicked on, hoping it would take some of the dampness out of the air.

In the upstairs storage room, she checked the inventory of cleaning supplies, paper products, shampoo and soap and made a few mental notes for her next order. Sometimes Martha and Alice reminded her about items they were running short on but sometimes they didn't.

By the time Harold finished his call, she had started to straighten the books on the shelves in the library. He came in to report the news. "My sister is on a respirator and her condition is deteriorating rapidly. I have to leave."

"I'm so sorry, Harold." She kissed his cheek. "Don't give up hope. I've seen many stroke cases that appeared severe at the onset but with treatment and therapy, a full recovery is possible, especially if she got to a hospital as soon as it happened."

"Well, she's a fighter. Always was."

"Good. That's important. The will to live can make all the difference in the world in a situation like this. Please call me when you can and let me know how she is."

"I can't say for sure when I'll be back, so go ahead and rent the room if you need to." His brow furrowed, and he took his glasses off to rub his eyes. "She's the last of my siblings, you know." That was all he could say.

Ellie gave him a long comforting hug. "Take care, Harold. I'll be thinking of you and will hope for the best. If there's anything I can do, please don't hesitate to call me."

He turned away from her then and went back to his room. He was packed and out the door before the last book was back in its proper place on the library shelf.

Downstairs, she wrote a note on Alice's clipboard advising her of Harold's sudden departure and the need to prepare his room for the next guest. Then she went into her apartment to call Wade.

"Ellie! You won't believe it!" he shouted when he recognized her voice.

She would like to have been able to see his face. He sounded like a different person, nothing like the man who was here the other night.

"What is it?"

"It's all gone. Burns, rash, everything! I look like nothing ever happened. Only thing is my hair is still, well, not so good. But my skin's not red now, and it doesn't hurt anymore."

"That's wonderful, Wade." She needed to hear some good news today. "It was Dr. Alexander's ointment, wasn't it?"

"I think so, yes. I'd already tried everything else I could think of and none of it helped. Exactly how did you make this stuff?"

Ellie ran through the directions, taking her time so he could write it all down.

"Now tell me, Ellie. How are things?"

That shouldn't have been a tough question to answer, but Ellie hesitated.

"That good, huh?"

"I don't know where to begin."

"Why don't we get together then? I'll come to the inn."

"I have a houseful of guests, Wade."

"Look, I know you don't want me to just drop in, so tell me what time to come."

"There really isn't a good time for you to come here. It's better if we meet somewhere."

"Sure. Okay. How about dinner?

"I'd rather not be away from the inn in the evening. Maybe I could get away for lunch while Alice and Martha are still here. Let's make it Monday."

"Okay then. I'll meet you at the diner on Monday at noon. We'll eat fast. I'll have to be back in time to teach my afternoon class anyway."

Ellie said goodbye, hung up and then called Fran. They made plans to go antiquing together a week from Sunday. Fran was working on a long four-part newspaper story right now about unemployment in eastern Pennsylvania and the loss of factory jobs. It was taking a lot of time. During the summer, they'd only had time for a quick cup of coffee together now and then. Both of them were looking forward to some time together to catch up.

After a quick supper of reheated leftovers, Ellie lit some candles in the parlor and with the fire building techniques she'd learned in Girl Scouts, she had a strong blaze going in the fireplace in no time. A few returning guests walked in the front door, rubbed their hands together and stood in front of it, remarking how good the fire felt.

Ellie had put out a winter beverage assortment and a pan of bread pudding that Martha had assembled earlier while Ellie was out. She whispered a soft thank you to her cook for having had the foresight to put together a much-appreciated warm dessert. All Ellie had to do was put it in the oven and then set it out on the table. Its aroma filled the entire downstairs of the inn and she loved it.

While the guests helped themselves, she sat at the kitchen table paging through some of the magazines that she hadn't had a chance to read and going through a stack of personal mail that had piled up over the past week. She didn't glance at the clock again until long after the last guest had turned in for the night and was surprised to see it was after ten. Time to clean up, spread what was left of the smoldering coals in the fireplace, and go to bed.

She stopped in the parlor doorway. A brilliant fire raged in the fireplace with tall yellow flames reaching to the top and sides of the opening. The kindling basket she'd brought home earlier in the day that had been filled with twigs and newspapers now stood empty.

Ellie raised her eyes toward Sally's portrait but was unable to read anything into the woman's expression. This didn't appear to be her doing.

Then she felt a slight breeze as if someone had brushed past her, but she could see no one there. The candle in the antique lantern on the end table flickered. She waited.

Soon Dr. Alexander's voice came to her through the familiar crackle of electricity in the air.

The fire had gone out and my men were cold.

She moved toward the mirror and watched a foggy mist spread from the center to the edges of the frame. Her sense of his presence felt stronger than ever and it excited her. "I'm sorry that I let it go out. I should have known that your men would be cold in this dampness."

You always understand. How is your hand, Ellen?

She smiled and looked down at the thin red slash on her finger. "Much better. Thanks to you, Dr. Alexander, it's almost healed."

You knew it was me, didn't you?

"At first I thought it was a dream. Then I saw the bandage that had come from your box of instruments, and I recognized the thread you used in the stitches."

If I'm to care for you properly while awaiting more casualties from the battlefield, I must have my instruments and supplies nearby. Where are they?

His words drove an aching stab of guilt into the pit of her stomach. This was why she'd felt so anxious in the shop this morning. The box of instruments didn't belong to her and she had no right to take them out of the house. Why hadn't she talked it over with him first?

"I'm sorry," she whispered. The mist took the shape of his now familiar face in the mirror as she spoke. "They're being repaired. Refurbished for you. I'll bring them back as soon as I can. Before the wounded come."

A long silence.

Very well, Ellen. They are in good hands then? To be returned soon?

"Yes. You may use mine until I'm able to return yours to you."

I would be most grateful.

"My medical kit is on the floor of the closet in my apartment."

Thank you.

Ellie thought she saw a faint smile on his misty face, but she probably just imagined it. She smiled back at him anyway. As she did so, his image sharpened. Still moving in the fog that surrounded him, the features of his face became clearer, especially his eyes. Large and filled with longing. She stepped close to the mirror and felt her heart beat faster as she brought her hand near the shiny surface, hoping for his touch.

"I wish I could see you better," she said. "Sometimes I can sense your presence. Other times I think you're near me, but you don't answer when I speak your name."

It's not always possible to answer. The hospital here takes up much of my time. So much of my treatment seems hopeless. I do everything I know how to do, and still my men bleed to death or die of fever and disease.

"You must not feel guilty, for anything. Even when you cannot cure, you provide comfort which is just as important. From what I've read and heard, you have a gift."

And what is this gift you believe I have?

"Your men write to their families and tell them what a fine doctor you are." Ellie was aware that she was speaking in present tense, but this conversation seemed perfectly normal to her. "They talk about how you share your rations with them and go without sleep when they need you. The gift, Dr. Alexander, is unselfish love for your fellow man. You give of yourself while asking nothing in return."

It seems that you are beautiful on the inside as well, Ellen. Words cannot express how much your thoughtfulness means to me. May I ask you to call me Grant?

"It would be my pleasure, Grant." She bowed her head.

When she lifted it, he was gone.

Expecting to wake up with the same foggy head she had experienced before when she'd been with Grant, Ellie was delighted to feel alert and energetic as soon as she opened her eyes. She showered and dressed in record time even before her first cup of coffee. Was it possible she was becoming accustomed to communicating with a spirit?

It was much more than that. She could hardly wait to be with him again and she couldn't stop smiling. No need to look in the mirror to see the glow that only comes from falling in love was plastered all over her face. She felt wonderful.

After the flurry of breakfast activity in the dining room followed by guest checkouts, Ellie gave instructions to her staff and left them to their work. She spent a few minutes at the computer and read the sad e-mail message that had just arrived from Harold. She wrote a long note in a card expressing her sympathy on the loss of his sister and added it to the stack of outgoing mail. Then she retreated to her apartment to get ready to run some errands.

Earlier, she'd thrown on her favorite pair of slacks and matching sweater, an outfit that was usually perfect for an autumn day. One glimpse in her full-length mirror told her it wasn't right.

Instead, she slipped into a crisp white long-sleeved blouse and tucked it into the waist of a long blue skirt. She couldn't remember the last time she'd worn either item but today they felt perfect, like something Grant was accustomed to seeing women wear. She hoped to find more outfits like this while she was in town. Anyone who saw her dressed in a long skirt like this might see her as a successful innkeeper and that certainly wasn't a bad thing.

On her way out, Ellie told Alice and Martha she'd be back well before they left for the day at 3:00 and had her cell phone along if they needed her. The short cold spell had given way to sunshine that warmed her shoulders as she strolled out to the car. She tossed a cardigan into the back seat out of habit and hoped she wouldn't need it.

Resting her elbows on top of the open car door, she lingered a moment to admire the inn and its grounds, sending a silent message of love to Aunt Carolyn. She filled her lungs with crisp autumn air.

Fred looked up and waved to her from the open door of the stone barn that towered over the back of the property. The tractor sat outside, ready for the final lawn cutting and more leaf cleanup. A small hinged door on the side of the tractor engine hung open. Ellie could make out some miscellaneous parts strewn on the pavement beside it, along with a can of motor oil. Fred loved that tractor. Sometimes she had to remind him to spend less time tinkering with it and focus more of his attention on the other chores at hand. Still, she couldn't ask for a more dependable worker. For as long as she'd known Fred, he'd never been faced with anything he couldn't fix, and he loved doing it.

She got into the car and turned it around in the parking area. As she headed out to the street, the lilac bush she'd planted at the front of the inn caught her eye. When was the last time she'd checked on it? The last thing she wanted was for her lilac to die from some plant disease when she wasn't paying attention. With all the rain this past week, she hadn't worried about watering outdoors, especially so late in the year.

Everything else she'd planted appeared to be thriving, so the lilac was probably doing fine. Still, she felt the need for a closer look just to make sure. The lilac was another connection to Grant and each one of them was precious.

A quick glance at her watch gave her permission. More than enough time to enjoy the yard before meeting Wade. She cut the engine, got out of the car, and walked across the front lawn, enjoying the gentle bounce from the soft grass beneath her feet.

Not only was the lilac bush doing well, it had grown to twice the size it was when she'd brought it home. Every leaf stood out, shining in the sunlight as if it had been polished during the night. A seasoned landscaper could not have trimmed it into a more perfect shape. It seemed to be thriving well in the spot where Grant told her to plant it. Smiling, Ellie reached out to touch one of the leaves, thinking how far her relationship with him had come since he first spoke to her.

A gentle breeze blew across the back of her hand like a soft caress and ruffled the tender branches. When she turned her head to feel the wind on her face, there was none. Wherever this breeze was coming from, it had a very limited range. The trees, the other shrubs, even the hair on her head remained still. Only the lilac rustled. There could be just one explanation. It was a reminder from Grant.

Her thoughts returned to the day she'd brought the lilac home and heard his voice inside her head, telling her where to plant it. Suppose she'd ignored his voice or been too frightened by it to do anything? The idea of not knowing Grant had become incomprehensible. His courage and dedication were greater than any doctor she'd ever known in her years at the hospital. Even in spirit, Grant remained a great man and she adored him.

She listened to the soft sound of the leaves brushing against one another and thanked him silently for all he'd brought into her life. The breeze sent a strong floral fragrance up toward her face, even though there were no flowers. Leaning over, she closed her eyes and pictured the blossoms that would appear here again in the spring. Another deep breath rewarded her with the sweetest of scents. Intoxicating.

Ellie arrived ten minutes early to find Wade waiting for her in a corner booth sipping a cup of coffee.

"Unbelievable!" Ellie exclaimed when she saw him. "I can't get over how much better you look. I know you said everything had healed but you look as if nothing ever happened. No wonder you were so excited when you called."

Wade responded with a proud smile, brighter than any expression she'd ever seen on his face. Running his hand above the surface of his stubbled head, he admitted that he wasn't a hundred percent back to normal. "Still need to grow some hair back," he said.

"It'll come, I'm sure."

"Coffee?" he asked as the server approached.

"No thanks. I'd like some chamomile tea, please."

"You look great, Ellie. Bit of a glow in your cheeks. Are you in love or something?"

She felt herself blush and looked away.

"I was just kidding but looks like I guessed right. Who is he?"

Ellie still didn't know what to say.

He studied her face, then pushed his coffee aside and leaned across the table. "Dr. Alexander." It was a statement, not a question. Wade was the only person in the world who would even suggest the possibility of falling in love with a spirit. Because it had happened to him too.

She found it very difficult to talk to Wade about Grant without letting on how thrilled she was. Unable to deny the truth now that he confronted her with it, she nodded.

"When you said that a lot had happened since I last saw you, I sure wasn't expecting this."

"Well, it's kind of hard to explain."

"You don't have to. I think I understand."

"Somehow I knew you would." As they looked across the table at each other with knowing expressions, Ellie felt another milestone passing by, another line crossed. Past irritations, suspicions and any other negative feelings she'd harbored toward Wade since they met had vanished. They shared a secret now that no one else could understand.

After ordering sandwiches, they made small talk until their lunch arrived.

"Now that you've told me how you feel about the doctor, I have something to confess to you."

She had no idea where he was going with this, but already regretted admitting how she felt about Grant. He might somehow use the intimate secret she'd just revealed and that was the last thing she wanted. If only her blush hadn't given it away.

"The other day when I came to the inn to see Sally's portrait, we talked about time travel. Remember?"

Ellie nodded, her mouth full of corned beef.

"Well, I tried it."

7

Ellie dropped her sandwich, ignoring the loose pieces of meat that bounced from her plate onto the table. With great effort, she was able to swallow without choking.

"Are you crazy?" She hadn't meant to shout, but it just came out that way.

"Of course not. Lower your voice."

How ironic. The same words she used on him in the restaurant the first time they went out together. In a loud whisper she said, "I knew you were toying with the idea, Wade, but I didn't believe you'd actually try it, especially after the fire and everything. Do you have a death wish or something?"

"I thought you knew more about the fire than you were letting on."

When she didn't answer, he pushed the issue a little more. "Tell me. How did you hear about it?"

"It was in the newspaper, remember?"

"Oh, yeah. Short article though."

"I can put two and two together as well as the next person."

"Okay. I'll admit my first attempt failed. Probably didn't have the time machine calibrated right. Something went wrong with my magnetic sensor and I didn't account for the constant friction it generated. That's what caused the burns. Well, the trouble could have been the result of any one of a hundred things. Anyway, that was months ago and I've learned a lot since then. How to keep from burning my skin, for one thing. Complicated business this time travel, but I'm not about to let that stop me from finding a way back to Sally."

"You didn't try to rebuild the machine, did you?"

"Gave up on that," he said, shaking his head. "After further research, I believe it's possible to travel in time without an actual machine."

Ellie put her elbows on the table and leaned forward, not wanting to miss a word. If Wade could travel back in time safely and successfully, then maybe she could too. The notion was outrageous and senseless, but she couldn't help getting excited.

Wade waited until the server confirmed they were finished, didn't want anything else, and left the check. Then he revealed a theory that left her speechless.

"Think about the story of Alice in Wonderland and her looking glass. Remember it?"

Ellie nodded. "All she had to do was climb into it and she emerged in another land. But that's a fairy tale, Wade. Just a story. People can't really do that."

"Yes, they can. Let me put it in simple terms."

"Please."

"Picture a tear in the fabric of our relationship with time here in the present and another tear in the past, a particular place at a particular time, leaving a sort of tunnel between them. The key is finding the entrance to the tunnel."

"It can't be that simple."

"It isn't simple at all, but I'm trying to keep it that way, so I can explain it to you."

"Okay. I'm still listening."

"This kind of thing creates sort of a closed loop in time, between the two gaps that are connected. I believe that Sally and Grant are using this to connect with us. To reach them, we have to use the tunnel they already established."

"Communicating with them is one thing. Traveling through time is quite another."

"Believe me, I know. Once you told me that Dr. Alexander communicates with you, it seemed like we could both get what we want."

"What do you mean?"

"Sally communicates with me through her portrait. You probably already figured that out."

"I wasn't sure until now, but it certainly appeared that way." Ellie finally understood Wade's obsession with the portrait on the wall that drove him to act the way he had since she first met him.

"So you see, Sally's portrait is my looking glass."

"And," Ellie whispered, "The mirror in the parlor is mine."

The following Sunday, Ellie picked Fran up for a few hours of antiquing. She was fifteen minutes late because she couldn't decide what to wear. She settled on a long forest green skirt and delicate print blouse, very similar to one in a photo she found in a book about women in the Civil War.

"Where are you going dressed like that?" Fran blurted out as soon as she shut the car door. "Do you want to borrow a pair of jeans?"

"No thanks. This is fine."

"Do you have an appointment somewhere later or what?"

"I just felt like wearing this, that's all." Rather than answer any more of Fran's pointed questions about her attire, Ellie changed the subject. "Any particular place you'd like to go today?"

"Interesting shops are all over these country roads, so it doesn't really matter which direction we go. It's just good to spend some time together. Besides, I never know when or where the next news story might crop up." They settled on a destination in the Amish country that Fran knew about but Ellie had never been to.

As usual, they wasted no time catching up with what was happening in each other's lives. They talked about Fran's money problems, Ellie's guests, the weather, and the latest town gossip, which brought the conversation around to Wade. Fran asked if Ellie had seen him lately, and Ellie admitted that they'd had lunch.

"You had lunch with him? What's the matter with you?"

"Nothing. He just called and wanted to talk. I didn't want anyone to see him coming into the inn or picking me up, so I met him at the diner."

Fran rolled her eyes. "So, what did he have to say? Anything I can put in the paper?"

"Fran, we agreed a long time ago that nothing I tell you goes into the newspaper unless you clear it with me first, right?"

"Of course." Fran sounded offended.

"Okay. Remember the fire at Wade's place?"

"Sure. He talked to you about that? At the time, he refused to tell me anything."

"Well, I don't print things in newspapers." Seeing the hurt look on Fran's face out of the corner of her eye, Ellie added, "I mean he probably figures it's safe to talk to me. Anyway, if I hadn't seen him in person I wouldn't have believed how good he looked."

"Wade Savage looked good? Ellie, what's gotten into you?"

They laughed at the absurd turn their conversation was taking. "I'd better explain. Remember the night we drank all that wine and things got so weird with Sally's portrait?"

"It gives me the willies every time I think about it."

"Me too. And remember the phone message from Wade asking to borrow the portrait?"

"Oh yeah. What ended up happening with that?"

"He came over the next day and spent some time with Sally's portrait and then decided he didn't need to borrow it after all. His burns were still pretty bad even after all that time."

"And?"

"He wanted to get together last week to show me how well he had healed."

"I have the feeling there's still something here you're not telling me."

"Dr. Alexander told me how to make an ointment for Wade's burns. We tried it and it really helped. Wade just wanted to show me the results."

"That's amazing. So, the doctor's still talking to you?"

Ellie smiled and nodded.

"Wow." After a long pause, Fran came back to life with more questions. "So back to Wade. What really happened the night of the fire? Did he tell you?"

Ellie looked over at her and back to the road again. "This stays between us, okay?"

"Okay, okay. I promise not to print anything. So, what did he say?"

"Well, it may have been the wine talking the night we moved the portrait, but I thought the fire might have been from some psychic connection he was trying to make with Sally."

Fran nodded. "And were you right?"

"Close. He built a time machine and was trying to travel back to the 1800s to be with Sally."

Fran snickered. "He's crazier than I thought. Did he really think he could do that?"

"Absolutely. He's still working on it. I couldn't understand much of what he was saying when he tried to explain it to me. Some intricate conglomeration of speed and mathematics and gravity. It was way over my head. Give me emergency medicine any day of the week."

"That's what makes my job as a reporter so good. Tell me anything and I can write about it." Fran laughed and waved her hand. "Just don't ask me to understand it." She reached into her purse for her cosmetic bag and applied another coat of dark red lipstick. "So why did Wade decide to tell you all this now?"

"After Dr. Alexander's remedy worked so well for him, Wade began to realize that the doctor and I have developed a kind of relationship." Ellie paused to choose her words carefully. Better not to raise any more red flags in Fran's mind. She didn't want to come across as strange as Wade even though she was finding herself moving in that direction more and more. "Wade just thought I'd be interested in his attempts to reach Sally."

"Hmm. I guess I could buy that. Tell me more about this 'relationship' you have with the doctor."

Ellie smiled. "I've had a few conversations with him since the last time you came to the inn."

"Dr. Alexander," Fran said. "The ghost with the voice. Hey, I forgot to ask you, how did things turn out with that great box of old instruments that you showed me?"

"Quite well so far, I think. Harold Lyster, the man I told you about? He recommended an antiques and restoration shop in Gettysburg. We took the box there a few weeks ago. When I checked on it yesterday, the shopkeeper said everything should be ready in a few more weeks."

"You trust the guy? I mean, that's valuable stuff you left with him. He sure is taking a long time."

"Believe me, I'm well aware of that."

"Don't get so touchy. I didn't mean anything by it."

"Sorry. It's just that," Ellie struggled to put her feelings into words. "It was so hard to let go of the box and leave it behind in the shop, you know? And then when I got home."

Fran interrupted with, "What?" as if that would make her talk faster.

"Dr. Alexander wanted to know where his instruments were. He said he would need them when the wounded men arrived."

"Golly." Fran slumped back in her seat.

"When I told him I was having them repaired and refurbished, he thanked me. I even offered him the use of my medical kit if he needed it before I brought his instruments back."

"Incredible."

Ellie turned into a parking area in front of a shop that had a big "Going Out of Business Sale" sign in the front window and turned off the engine. She wanted to tell Fran about the dressing on her finger the night she cut it on the broken wine glass, but she reconsidered. It might be too much for her friend to absorb all at once. Fran really looked stunned.

"Do you want to sit in the car all afternoon or shall we go inside?" Ellie teased.

Fran laughed and followed her into the shop. The prices were low, but the store was half empty, and Ellie didn't find many quality items left. She wandered over to the jewelry display and leaned over the glass case while Fran zeroed in on some old books about local history.

A beautiful cameo brooch stood out among the rest of the pins and necklaces on display. The graceful silhouette of a woman framed in rose gold rested on a cushion of black velvet. She asked the woman behind the counter to show it to her. As soon as she touched it, the cameo seemed to come to life in her hand with soft but distinct electrical energy. Ellie would have taken it home no matter what the asking price. The fact that it was a real bargain was immaterial.

When the woman started to wrap it, Ellie surprised herself by saying, "No, don't do that. I'll wear it." As soon as she pinned it to the front of her blouse, she felt its warmth through the fabric. She stared at her reflection in the small mirror on the counter, her eyes focused only on the brooch and she whispered, "Perfect".

Fran touched her shoulder, breaking the spell. "What'd you buy?"

When Ellie turned to face her, Fran said, "It's pretty but doesn't exactly go with most of your clothes. Are you sure you want to wear it? I mean, it's an antique, right?"

"It may not match most of my things but goes with what I have on today. In fact, I'll probably be wearing more of this and less of my older things. It's just right for the hostess of a historical inn, don't you think?"

Fran shrugged. "Well, we've got about an hour left before we have to start heading back." She was familiar with Ellie's schedule and knew her three o'clock curfew was not negotiable.

"I've used my spending allowance for the day on this little book about the Battle of Hanover." Fran waved her book in the air on the way to the car. "Most people never heard of it. Everybody knows Gettysburg, but nobody knows Hanover."

"Looks like an interesting book. Could I borrow it when you're finished?" Ellie asked, slowing the car to a halt at the edge of the shop driveway.

"Sure."

"Right or left?"

"Your call. I can browse anywhere without buying."

"Okay. One more stop I'd like to make. Isn't there a big general store sort of a place out this way?"

Fran gave her some approximate directions and after a few wrong turns, they found it. Once inside, Fran announced that it was a rather inexpensive book she'd bought and maybe there was enough left in her budget for something small at the candy counter.

Ellie went straight to the cosmetics section and looked up and down the aisle through the bubble baths and lotions, unable to find what she was looking for.

After Fran completed her purchase, she wandered down the same aisle from the opposite direction and held a white bag under Ellie's nose. "Lemon drop?"

"No thanks," Ellie responded without even looking inside the bag.

Fran followed Ellie's gaze from her face to the shelves in front of them and asked through a mouthful of candy, "Planning on taking a bath or something?"

"Not exactly. Ah, there it is." Ellie picked up a tester bottle of lilac water and sprayed some on her forearm. She inhaled deeply.

"If I didn't know you better, I'd say you were getting high on that stuff. Look at that smile on your face. Here, give me a whiff of that." Fran brought Ellie's wrist to her nose and sniffed. "Smells like flowers," she said.

"Exactly." Ellie took the two remaining bottles from the shelf and carried them to the cash register without further explanation.

Fran rode home with the passenger side window all the way open. "It's a nice smell, Ellie, but it's giving me a headache."

"Sorry. I'll go easy on it from now on."

"Since when did you start wearing lilac perfume?"

"Since today."

Fran raised one eyebrow but said nothing more about it.

Assuring her friend that she'd enjoyed their time together, Ellie dropped Fran off and continued home, dipping into her bag only once to add a little more lilac water to her skin.

Ellie stayed busy keeping her paperwork and errands caught up before it was time for the holiday season to begin. After the bank deposit was ready to go and her accounting entries for the end of the month were posted, she took a few minutes to sit back to admire her strong bottom line. She had plenty of cash set aside now to get serious about moving forward with her renovation plans after the new year.

"I'll never be the innkeeper that you were, Aunt Carolyn," she said in her softest voice. "But you taught me well and I love you for it."

A sparkle at the rim of one of Aunt Carolyn's etched wine glasses winked at her from the china cabinet. Not much of a response, but it was enough to convince Ellie that her message got through. She winked back, tidied up the desk and turned her thoughts to the holidays.

When the phone rang, Ellie was delighted to hear the voice of the man from the restoration shop. Her precious box of instruments was ready for her to pick up. He was sure she would be pleased with the result. How many times had she heard him say those words? She'd soon find out how true they were.

When she walked into the shop an hour later, the box of instruments was nowhere in sight. She rang the tingly bell on the counter and waited. When the shopkeeper emerged from behind the curtain at the back of the main room and saw her, he held up one finger and disappeared again. He returned carrying the box out in front of him as if it contained the crown jewels. "Here we are," he announced and placed it on the counter for her inspection and approval.

They examined each item one at a time and Ellie was indeed pleased with everything he had done. He'd even cleaned the dark red velvet lining, which brought out its original color and added a soft luster. She couldn't wait for Grant to see it.

Tonight would be a special occasion that warranted a special dress. Bolstered by the inn's solid month-end financial position, Ellie decided to stop at the period clothing store where the living history people and re-enactors shopped. Just to look around.

It didn't take her long to find the perfect dress: a matching bodice and floor length skirt made of polished cotton in soft lavender, the color of lilacs that set off the blue in her eyes. The white lace collar and matching cuffs added a touch of elegance. The skirt swirled around her ankles as she turned full circle in front of the mirror in the fitting room. Her new cameo belonged at the neckline of this dress.

The weight of this clothing surprised her, and she needed instructions for getting into it. By the time she'd added the proper undergarments to her ensemble, the total price seemed extravagant, especially for something that no one else besides Grant would likely ever see. It didn't matter. She had to have it.

That night, after all the guests had turned in and the remains of hot spiced tea and Martha's gingerbread were cleared away, it was time to get ready.

Ellie turned out the parlor lights and lit several candles, creating the perfect atmosphere. She hadn't been able to sit still since she'd brought the dress home. It took up a lot of space in her bedroom closet, but she made room for it by bagging up some of the New York clothes that she never expected to wear again and storing them.

It wasn't easy dressing by herself that night. She'd managed but it took a lot longer than it did in the shop when she had assistance. Taming her wild curls into submission also took more of an effort than she anticipated, but the end result made it all worthwhile. Parted in the center now, her hair was smooth and confined into a tight roll across the sides of her head to the nape of her neck where she pinned it up close to her head. Then she added the cameo and a touch of lilac water.

When she faced her reflection in the mirror, her vision blurred from the soft misty tears that welled in her eyes. The total change in her appearance was wonderful and it felt so right. She hoped the effect on Grant would be the same.

Lifting the instrument box from the floor of the closet, she wondered if he'd been able to see her bring it in the back door. Was it possible to hide something from a spirit that roamed your house? She had no idea but soon it wouldn't matter.

She tiptoed into the parlor with the box in her arms and waited. Soon, thick white mist erupted from the mirror, swirled around her and returned, forming a distinct image of the face she'd come to love. His mouth shifted into a soft smile.

Ellen. How lovely you are tonight.

"I was hoping you would be pleased."

Indeed I am.

She held the box out toward the mirror. "Your instruments," she said, opening the polished wooden lid.

A faint wisp of white floated in front of her and she watched the instruments move out of the box, turn in the air and settle back in their places again, one at a time.

This is remarkable indeed. They look brand new.

"Shall we keep them together with my medical kit?" she asked.

Excellent idea. I'll know where to find them when the next wagonload of wounded arrives. How may I possibly repay your kindness?

"There is no need. When one cares deeply for another…" she lowered her head, embarrassed.

As I care for you, Ellen. More than my words can express.

She set the box down and waited with her arms out-stretched to welcome him, unable to calm the pounding of her heart. The electricity in the air was nearly unbearable. She couldn't catch her breath.

The brooch on the front of her dress moved just slightly as he touched it, but she couldn't see his hand. She could hear his voice and his footsteps and feel his touch where she stood but could only see him through the mirror.

My mother wore a brooch exactly like this one, Ellen. How did you know?

She murmured something. Then his hand slid across to her shoulder and he brought her to him. Ellie closed her eyes and melted into his warm embrace. This was the moment she'd been longing for. She lay her head on his shoulder, gently at first, and then rubbed her cheek against the rough wool of his uniform. His hands moved across her back and he held her close.

Hmm. The scent of lilac. It has been such a very long time.

"Grant, when I close my eyes, you seem so real to me, your touch so solid and firm. And yet…"

I know, my dearest. But I remain of another time far removed from yours. There is nothing either of us can do to change that.

When she brought him even closer to her body, she felt his response against her and it excited her more. His beard brushed her face when she turned her head, seeking his lips. Their kiss was unlike any other, almost magical. His embrace gave her the sensation of floating above the floor, swirling with him in the mist, the two of them together as one. Too soon, her feet touched the carpet again, and he took her hands.

Her arms stretching out in front of her, she imagined he must be looking at her now from head to toe, although she still couldn't see him clearly. She closed her eyes and pictured him, putting together the details from the face that he'd shown to her in the mirror with those she'd touched with her fingertips, memorizing everything.

He let go of one hand and held the other in both of his. She felt his kiss on the back of her hand, then the softness of his beard as he held her palm to his cheek.

Good night, my dearest.

Oh no. Not yet. "So soon?"

I must check on my men. It is well past time for my rounds.

"Until tomorrow, then."

The mist faded before her eyes. Knowing his departure was inevitable didn't stop her from reaching out to grasp what little remained of him before he was gone. She stood alone in the parlor like Cinderella after the ball was over, not wanting to take off this dress or wash her hands and face.

Grant's footsteps began at the bottom of the stairs and she heard them climb one at a time until he reached the upstairs hall to make his rounds. The footsteps faded, dimmed by voices of men moaning and crying out in pain. She strained to hear Grant's gentle voice comforting them as he moved back and forth across the floor above.

Then the sound of his boots grew louder again. He was returning to the stairs. She held her breath hoping he'd come back to her even though they'd already said goodnight. One footstep on top stair and then on the next one, each a little louder. He was coming down. Her heart raced. She waited at the bottom, expecting a glimpse of white mist floating around the corner. But when the footsteps reached the landing, they stopped.

She rushed back to the parlor, hoping to see some sign of him again. All she saw was the angry image of Sally Brendel scowling at her from above the fireplace.

The next morning, Alice approached Ellie after the guests had departed for their daily excursions. It was a rare sunny day in November. Martha had gone into town for groceries and supplies and Fred was outside pounding nails into sections of the old split rail fence that had come loose during a recent storm.

"Could I talk to you a minute, Ellie?" Alice asked, wiping her hands on a dishtowel.

"Of course." Ellie poured two cups of fresh coffee and carried them over to the kitchen table where they sat opposite each other. She sipped, waiting for Alice to say what was on her mind. Sometimes it took a while.

"I've been hearing things from the guests off and on for some weeks now and thought to myself that it's probably time to say something to you about it."

"I always want to know what our guests are saying about Ivy Garden, good or bad. Don't ever hesitate to tell me."

"When I'm helping Martha with the breakfast, you know, I hear the guests talking while I'm serving them."

She nodded, waiting for Alice to get to the point. Ever since she'd burned the pancakes, Ellie stayed out of the way and left the breakfast tasks to her staff who often picked up feedback from her guests while she was at the front desk.

"Almost every day at least one of them will say something about the noises they heard upstairs during the night."

"What kind of noises?"

"Loud footsteps mostly. Out in the hall or on the stairs. But sometimes it's more. Men moaning and groaning. Strange sounds they can't quite make out. Do you hear them too?"

"My bedroom is in the back corner of the house, you know, on the other side of the kitchen. I usually tidy up out here around ten and then go to bed.

"Pretty sound sleeper, are you?"

"Most of the time."

"You sure you don't hear anything?"

"Maybe it's coming from other guests moving around in their rooms. These old floors tend to creak."

"That's what I thought, too. But last night when the Fletchers were our only guests and they said they heard the noises too. I heard them asking each other who might have been walking around the guest rooms in the middle of the night if no one else was staying here."

So Ellie wasn't the only one who could hear Grant moving around at night amid the cries of wounded men. She hadn't realized others could hear them too. What could she possibly do about it?

"You say this happens every night?"

"Yes. Almost every morning somebody has something to say about it at breakfast."

"Thank you for telling me about this, Alice. I'll pay close attention and see if I can figure out what's happening. Please let me know if you hear anything more about it."

Alice stayed in her chair, hands on the table fidgeting. Obviously, she had something else on her mind. After a few minutes, she spoke. "I hope you don't mind my saying this, Ellie, this being your home and everything, but…"

"Whatever it is, Alice, please don't be afraid to speak up. Ivy Garden is my home, that's true. It's also where you come to work every day, so if there's something bothering you we should talk about it."

This appeared to make sense to Alice. "Lately, I've heard some guests talking that maybe the inn is haunted."

Ellie wasn't sure what to say next.

"They were talking about ghosts, I mean."

"Did they sound like they were afraid? Or that they might not come back?"

"I don't think so, no. As a matter of fact, they sounded more like they were excited about the possibility. I just wanted you to know what folks are saying. If it was one or two I wouldn't mention it, but this talk of ghosts seems to be going on all the time now. That's all I wanted to tell you."

Ellie mulled this over. She supposed it was bound to happen but wasn't sure how she felt about running "The Haunted Ivy Garden Inn".

"Ellie, have you ever felt like someone was watching you but when you turn around you can't see anyone there?"

"Yes, I have. Most of my life at one time or another."

"It happens to me too but only when I'm here. No place else."

"Try not to let it bother you. It's fairly common." She hesitated then asked, "Do you believe in ghosts, Alice?"

"Me?" She thought for a moment. "No. There's no such thing." She stood up and waved her dishtowel, dismissing the idea. "People just like to talk." Alice wandered out of the kitchen, muttering to herself.

A week later, just before locking up and going to bed, Ellie watched a car turn off the road and roar up the driveway. The driver got out and ran up toward the door. The lanterns on the porch illuminated the face of Wade Savage.

Ellie unbolted the front door and swung it open. "What's the matter with you, driving in here like a maniac? I thought we agreed you wouldn't come here again."

"Fine greeting," he said, stepping in past her without waiting for an invitation.

What was it with this guy? Either he was polite and understanding, or rude and inconsiderate. It was obvious which Wade Savage had just crossed her doorstep. "What do you want?"

"Need to see Sally. Won't stay long. Promise."

The damage was already done. Myra and George Keller must have heard his car pull in and no doubt rushed to their window to see who it was, even if that meant getting out of bed to look. They didn't miss a thing.

"Well, here she is," Ellie said, gesturing toward the portrait. She switched on the lights that she had just turned off a few minutes earlier. Now that she could see Wade in brighter light, she realized how tired and disheveled he looked. Downright scary, in fact. She rubbed her nose. He needed a shower and some deodorant too. Dramatic change from the finicky eccentric he was when she first met him.

"What have you been doing?" she asked.

"Struggling to get back to Sally. Nothing's gone right. I just want her to know how hard I've tried." He collapsed on the sofa opposite the fireplace and stared in silence at Sally's face. To Ellie, the portrait appeared normal, but she wasn't making much of an effort to examine it closely. Too busy fuming at Wade's poorly timed and inconsiderate visit.

"Is Sally supposed to forgive you for taking so long?"

He didn't answer.

"Wade, it's late. I'm tired. Do you plan to sit here all night watching the portrait or take it home or what?" She stood in front of him with her arms out at her sides, palms upward and resorted to waving them to get his attention when he didn't answer.

"Can't do that. Told you before. She belongs here."

The steely edge to his voice told Ellie not to argue. She sat down in her chair by the window and watched Wade watch Sally. His facial expressions alternated between humility and eagerness. It was obvious who had the upper hand in that relationship.

Wade. Sally asked me to speak to you.

8

Grant's voice startled both of them. They looked at each other, then around the room. No swirling mist, just a white haze across the mirror.

"It's Dr. Alexander, isn't it?" Wade asked, grinning now. He leaned toward Ellie and spoke in a conspiratorial whisper, "This is terrific!"

Clearing his throat first, he addressed Grant. "Dr. Alexander. This is Wade Savage speaking. I…"

I know very well who you are, Wade. No need to announce yourself.

"Oh, okay. Well…"

Ellie was enjoying Wade's imitation of the Cowardly Lion standing before the Great and Powerful Oz. She sat back in her chair and hugged herself. Everything's okay, she thought. Grant's still here.

Sally wants you to bring her forward. Into your present time.

"Why? I've been trying to go back to 1863. Back to her."

And you're not succeeding, are you?

"No, but I intend to keep working on it."

Perhaps the time has come to try something different.

"Any suggestions on how I might do that?"

That would be entirely up to you.

"Great." That took the wind out of his sails. "By the way, I'd like to thank you for the ointment you helped Ellie make for me. It worked."

I see that it has. Except for your hair, it seems.

"I know." He touched his head. "It starts to grow, then falls out again."

Use equal parts of brandy and strong black tea, shaken well together. Rub into the roots of the hair once daily.

"Will it work as well as the ointment?"

As long as you are careful not to scratch or irritate the scalp with rough combing or brushing. Allow it to heal.

Enough medical consultation. "Grant, how well do you know Sally?" Ellie asked.

Wade's head whirled around, his face furious at first.

Ellie glared back at him.

He relaxed then, evidently seeing the wisdom in this line of questioning.

I have stayed here at Sally's home since the great battle, tending to the many wounded.

136

"Then you've spent a lot of time with her."

Yes, I have. It was not Sally's choice to open her home. The Union Army has the right to commandeer property whenever and wherever it sees fit. During those first few days, the wounded and dying filled her beds, every spot on the floor and spilled out onto the porch and into the yard. Conditions are somewhat improved now.

Ellie had known this but hearing it in Grant's words made it seem more real. She looked around her parlor, into the dining room, and through the window to the front porch, empty and still in the soft lantern light, and pictured this place as Grant described.

"She works hard for you and your men," Wade said.

Indeed she does. The sacrifices of war are many, for those who fight as well as for those who remain at home. Sally has given to the Union more than many women have. We are very grateful to her. She is rather resentful, however, and often becomes restless and bitter. Wade, Sally has expressed to me that she prefers to be with you, in your place in time, primarily because her life here has become so difficult under these trying circumstances. This house will remain unsettled until you take her away from the endless misery of the life she leads here.

"You're the cause of all her misery, you know. You rejected her when you knew she was fond of you. You and your Army destroyed her home and then left her with nothing. No food, no livestock, and no means to survive. Can you blame her for wanting to escape?" Wade's voice grew louder.

"Quiet, Wade. Please. The people upstairs are sleeping."

Thank you, Ellen. You understand how very precious sleep can be for those in pain. We must give the wounded every opportunity to rest whenever possible. I must leave you now and see to their comfort.

"Dr. Alexander, I'm not done talking to you yet."

Grant didn't answer.

"It doesn't work that way, Wade. He comes and goes on his terms, not yours or mine."

"Apparently." He slid down onto the sofa cushions, recovering from the encounter. His legs hung over the arm at the end.

Ellie made a mental note to brush and freshen the entire sofa in the morning.

"So how does he expect me to bring Sally here? I haven't been able to figure out how to travel through time myself yet."

"Wade, you're a college professor. You'll figure it out." With that, she opened the front door for him and he left.

The next morning when Ellie's cell phone rang, she recognized the caller ID of the attorney and picked it up. Although he had given her preliminary information weeks ago related to the settlement of Aunt Carolyn's estate, he wanted to go over everything with her and sign the papers. Aunt Carolyn had added her to the title of the property and all of her accounts long ago, so this was a mere formality. They agreed to meet at nine on the following Monday. She called Fran to see if they could get together while Ellie was in town.

Unfortunately, her appointment with the attorney would eat up the most of her morning and she had other errands to run. Fran would be tied up later. They settled for some catch up time over lunch later in the week. Fran would call to confirm. They promised to make time for each other no matter how cluttered their schedules were.

After the daily flurry of guest checkout and a quick review of what Martha and Alice needed to do today, Ellie had just enough time to change clothes and get to her appointment. Not a good idea to keep an attorney waiting. Especially an expensive one.

She rarely wore slacks around the inn anymore, keeping instead to the long skirts and modest blouses she knew Grant liked to see her wear. It was important to look right for him whether she knew he could see her or not. No matter what she wore, her outfit always included the antique cameo and a splash of lilac water. Today, however, she decided a pair of dress pants and a jacket would make getting in and out of the car easier and keep her long skirts from dragging in the early winter snow that had fallen overnight.

The roads were worse than she expected. The appointment got off to a bad start, even though she'd only missed their agreed upon time by ten minutes. The attorney had postponed this meeting several times. The legal red tape required to settle an estate seemed endless to Ellie. It gave her a new appreciation for the ordeal that the families she'd come to know at the hospital went through when a loved one died. At least she wasn't faced with financial problems resulting from the long drawn out process. Still, there had to be an easier way to streamline an inheritance than the path this lawyer was leading her down. Finally, everything had been put into her name only instead of both hers and Aunt Carolyn's. After today, all the loose ends would be tied up. The good news was that Aunt Carolyn had left her a larger inheritance than she ever imagined.

By the time she left the law office, her head was pounding, and her shoulders ached from the tension. The entire process left her feeling exhausted and depressed. All she wanted to do was go home, lie down for a while and have a good cry.

Fortunately, the inn was quiet when she returned and the only message on her answering machine was for Fred. Something about delivering a load of shingles for an emergency repair of the barn roof. She wrote down the number and pinned it to the bulletin board by the back door where her staff left notes for each other. A very basic system, but it worked well for them.

On the first Saturday of December, Fred brought in a lovely fresh pine tree and set it up in the corner of the parlor. Ellie thoroughly enjoyed decorating the inn for Christmas. Aunt Carolyn always had it finished before Ellie arrived on Christmas

Eve and Ellie never bothered to decorate her apartment in New York. Martha and Alice helped with the decorations and didn't hesitate to remind Ellie where certain things had to be placed, always the same every year. It took all four of them a full day.

When they finished admiring how beautiful everything looked, Ellie sent them home and sat down to look over Martha's menus for the holidays. Martha often shopped at Amish markets to get freshest food items for the inn. Ellie never ceased to be impressed by the quality of what she brought back no matter what the season and was even more impressed with how creative she was with her recipes. There was no end to the variations of toppings for pancakes, waffles and French toast that Martha could put together.

Ellie had heard through the Bed and Breakfast grapevine that Martha was occasionally wooed by other inns in the area. Her solid reputation as an excellent cook was well known around town and beyond. Fortunately for Ellie, Martha remained loyal and there was no doubt that her tasty breakfasts and evening desserts kept many of their guests returning.

As the end of the year approached, there were fewer and fewer reservations, except for the rush of people who came to attend the holiday events around Gettysburg. Tree lightings, carriage rides and Christmas balls always attracted tourists, although Ellie had trouble understanding why they didn't want to be at home at this time of year. She was always grateful to have guests at the inn, but she wondered why these people weren't spending the holidays with their friends and families.

Late on New Year's Eve, the inn was empty and Ellie sat alone in the parlor, sipping mulled wine and longing for Grant. Where was he? Didn't he know that Christmas had come and gone? Ellie hadn't seen or heard anything from Grant in weeks. He could have moved out for all she knew. Although she felt frustrated and a little worried that maybe she had been dreaming all of it, she kept telling herself he'd make his presence known when he was ready, just as he had since she'd known him. Most of the time, she was content to have the few moments he could spare. Tonight, none of that made her feel any better.

After the rush of holiday events and house parties ended, an unexpected cloud of loneliness surrounded her. It was her first Christmas season without Aunt Carolyn that she could remember and she was trying hard to get through it without becoming depressed. When the tears started, she scolded herself for allowing self-pity to creep in and went to bed.

Once the door to her apartment closed behind her, Ellie allowed her tears to fall. They rolled into sobs that shook her entire body. "Aunt Carolyn, I miss you so much. I've tried to do everything the way you would have wanted me to but it's not enough. Why didn't I come to live with you sooner? I was so selfish, so foolish to think my job was more important! It's my fault you were here by yourself and died all alone. Now it's too late. It'll always be too late."

She wasn't alone, Ellen.

"Grant!" She sank into a heap on the bed, covered her face with her hands and cried even harder. "Oh Grant, I feel so guilty!"

Her sobs slowed when she felt him sit down beside her on the bed, causing the mattress sink down enough for her to see the depression of his weight in the surface of the bedspread. But that's all she saw. No mist, no swirl of movement. She welcomed the familiar electricity in the air. It meant he was here to console her and that was all that mattered.

She felt his arm around her as he drew her close. Her head found its way to his shoulder and she nestled into him for comfort. Holding each other, they lay back, side by side on the bed. His hand stroked the back of her head, soothing her. When he drew her even closer, she closed her eyes, picturing him beside her.

I was here with her when she died.

"Oh, Grant. That means so much to me, to know she wasn't truly alone that day. Did she suffer very much? Please tell me she didn't."

The end came swiftly. I tried to help her, Ellen. You must believe that I did what I could.

"Of course. The same as you do for everyone."

Yes. I know you truly loved her. She loved you too, Ellen, just as much. I hope you believe that.

"I know she loved me, Grant. I just wish…"

Shhh. It is not our place to question destiny. It was her time to leave. There was nothing anyone could have done to prevent that. Not even you, Ellen.

She lay still in his arms, thinking about what he'd said. "It's so hard for me to see it that way. Nurses are trained to save lives, not let them go."

So are doctors. That is why we find it so difficult to accept that we cannot control everything that happens in our lives. But some of it is beyond our ability. As it should be.

His hand moved from the back of her head to the side of her face. He brushed away the last of her tears with a gentle kiss on each of her cheeks in a comforting yet sensual gesture.

She rubbed her face against the palm of his hand and turned to kiss it. His responding caress quickened her heart. As long as she kept her eyes closed, Ellie could allow herself to believe Grant was real. He felt so strong and solid. Keeping her eyes closed, she turned and buried her face in his beard above the rough wool of his uniform.

His rapid breathing rushed into her ear as his hand moved down over her shoulder. They began to move together in a choreographed ballet. Oh, how she wanted him. How she needed him. She raised her head, hungry for his kiss.

A distant bell rang in her ears. No matter how hard she tried to ignore it, it grew louder.

Then she woke up.

Oh no. It couldn't have been a dream. He was here, and he was real, and she wanted him back. She stood up and turned full circle beside the unmade bed and looked down on the two depressions side by side on the bed where she and Grant held each other. No, it wasn't a dream.

A quick glance in the mirror told her she wasn't ready to face anyone at the door. What a sight. Swollen eyes, streaked face. Her flattened curls lay plastered against her head on one side and stuck out in wild angles on the other.

The ringing doorbell at the front stopped but it was replaced by persistent pounding at the back. Opening the door just a crack, she called out, "Who is it?"

"Ellie?"

Wade Savage. She should have guessed.

"I'm not feeling very well, Wade. I'll call you later."

"It's important. Just give me a few minutes."

With Wade, it was always important. "Okay. Wait for me in the kitchen." She didn't want him scaring off any new guests who might wander in today before they had even registered. Better to keep him out of sight.

"Right."

She closed the door, wanting to delay becoming Ellie again for as long as she could. In her mind, she replayed everything Grant had said to her, reliving every moment of his visit. Her fingers traced all the places where he'd touched her, reluctant to let his loving embrace to slip away.

In the bright light of the bathroom, she looked even worse. It took her more than a few minutes to redo her hair and put on some makeup, but she finally made herself presentable.

"Thought you said a few minutes," Wade said as she came into the kitchen.

"I have a terrible headache, Wade. What's so important?"

"Sit down. There's been a breakthrough."

Ellie raised her eyebrows at that and the movement hurt her head. She rubbed her hand across her forehead to ease the pain. Out here in the kitchen, it was even brighter than the bathroom. With one hand across her brow to shield her sensitive eyes from the sun's glare, she tried to focus on Wade's face. It took tremendous effort and she wasn't sure it was worth it.

Over Wade's shoulder, she could see Myra Keller through the back window. She was standing in her driveway, elbows bent with one fist on each hip, glaring. Ellie looked away, hoping it was too cold for her to stay out long. The next time she looked, Myra had already spun around and was marching back toward her house.

Wade didn't seem to notice. Why should he? Myra wouldn't be knocking on his door to complain about the company he kept.

"Went up to take a look at that third-floor room while I was waiting."

Sally had lived alone on the third floor in very austere surroundings after her husband died. With her furnished rooms rented out after the war for the income she desperately needed, Sally had no choice but to spend the remainder of her life in the only place left, upstairs from the strangers who slept in the rooms that had once been her own.

Aunt Carolyn had talked about renovating the third floor but just never got around to it. After the holidays, Ellie immersed herself in her plans to turn the entire floor into a suite. Aunt Carolyn left her with a lot more than she ever dreamed possible and except for the harshest part of winter, business was good.

Ellie started lining up contractors to create the perfect suite that included a large sitting room with a fireplace, a sunny bedroom with a king sized bed and spa bath. She would have to be careful not to allow the construction to affect her guests any more than necessary.

Of course, Wade was sure he knew how Sally would want it to look and didn't hesitate to pass those desires along to Ellie. Although, they didn't always agree on the right balance between authenticity and comfort. They'd gone back and forth with ideas for weeks and the resulting plans were shaping up to please them both.

"I was thinking of hanging Sally's portrait above the fireplace in the suite, since that was her room." She didn't want him all bent out of shape if the next time he came, she'd already moved it upstairs.

"No! That's the worst thing you can do. Her portrait has a place of honor down in the parlor. It signifies to everyone who comes in that she's the lady of the house. She'd see it as a demotion. You don't want to do that, Ellie. Believe me."

"Okay, okay. It was just an idea."

"A bad idea."

"Spare me the lecture Wade," Ellie said, not caring how rude she sounded. "I feel terrible and I have a million things to do. Did you come here just to give your final approval to my plans for the suite or what?"

"No. Something else. Last time I was here, Grant talked to me, remember?"

"He talked to us, actually."

He chose to ignore that. "And Grant said that Sally wanted to live with me in the present, right?"

"What are you getting at?"

"I've spent months trying to get back to Sally. Back to the 1860s. I built a time machine, but it blew up. I rebuilt it. It blew up again, only not so bad the second time."

"And your point is…"

"My calculations, all the research, and discussions I've had with others who have tried it, everything points me toward the same principle."

"Which is?" What a grueling conversation this was turning into. It was like playing charades with an engineer. One she didn't even want to talk to in the first place.

"Exchange."

"I'm sorry, Wade, but I'm not getting any of this. My head is pounding, I feel like throwing up, and you're not making any sense. Could we do this some other time?"

"No. I need your answer now."

"I don't recall the question." She could see he was getting impatient with her. This was a good sign. Maybe there was a chance this conversation could come to an end and he would leave. Soon.

"I'm coming to that. Just let me finish."

"Make it quick."

"In order for Sally to move forward into present time, an exchange is required. Otherwise, she leaves a void in the past that can't be filled. It's all about speed and gravity and time and space, like I explained to you before. Too complicated to get into it any deeper than that right now, since you're in a hurry."

At least he'd heard her say that much. "So, you send something back when Sally comes forward," she said.

He looked into her face as if seeing her for the first time.

"Not something. Someone. You."

During the hours after he said them, those words echoed in her head again and again. At first it seemed inconceivable to her that Wade thought he would be able to send her back in time and bring Sally forward. But what was even more unbelievable was that she really wanted to go. In fact, she could think of nothing else.

Ellie had no idea how long she'd been daydreaming that afternoon but found herself holding a pillow from the parlor sofa in her hand, staring at the mirror when she realized it was dark outside. By the time she went to bed, she was even thinking about how to put her affairs in order because she didn't expect to ever be back.

A good night's sleep helped put things back into perspective but didn't erase the possibility of time travel from her mind. She planned to squeeze in a trip to the library for some books on time travel as soon as she could. Books that put the concept into plain English, which was something beyond Wade's capability. She couldn't go into this without some idea of what to expect.

By spring, reservations were starting to pick up again. Warmer weather and clearer skies were on their way. Ellie sat at her desk, making sure the reservations made for the coming week were in order.

One name jumped out at her from the computer screen. A famous author was scheduled to arrive at the end of the week. Unlike arrangements made by phone, online reservations always went straight into the system, so she didn't always know who was coming until she made it a point to review them. She never expected to see a name like this: Warren Blake.

Fran would love to interview him for the newspaper, she thought. It was worth a phone call to see if he'd be interested. To her surprise, he answered his own phone. Didn't famous authors have assistants who did that for them?

After a little small talk under the pretense of calling to confirm his reservation, she casually brought up the idea of an interview. He agreed and even said he'd look forward to it.

She called Fran to give her the exciting news.

"Hey, Ellie!" Fran's cheery voice always lifted Ellie's spirits regardless of her state of mind.

"How are you, Fran?"

"Ornery as ever." After some small talk, Fran asked, "Say, I never heard how that box of instruments turned out? Did you finally get it back?"

"Oh, the shopkeeper did a beautiful job. They look brand new. The box, the lining, everything. I'm delighted."

"Can't wait to see them. Did he frame them for you, like we talked about doing?"

Ellie had forgotten all about Fran's recommendation. She couldn't lock Grant's instruments away in a display case. Her long pause gave Fran the obvious answer.

"It's okay if you didn't. I mean, it's not like you were doing it for me."

"I just decided to keep them the way I found them. In the box."

"What will you do with the box?"

"Just keep it."

"Oh. Okay."

"I have some good news for you, my friend."

"I can use it. My rent check bounced this morning."

"Ooh, sorry to hear that."

"Good thing I have an understanding landlord. So far, anyway."

"Let's hope it stays that way. Listen, I wanted to tell you we have a famous guest coming a week from Monday. An author."

"Really? Who is it?"

"Warren Blake."

"You've got to be kidding."

"Not only is he staying here at Ivy Garden, but he's already agreed to give you an interview for the newspaper. I just asked him."

"You're an angel. Thanks a million."

Ellie could hear the smile in her friend's voice. "You have about ten days to plan what to say to him. Make the most of it."

"It will take me ten days to get ready, believe me. I might even splurge on a new pantsuit. Something to make me look professional. What do you think?"

"Good idea. But before you spend your hard-earned money on a brand new one, I just went through my closet a while ago and downsized my wardrobe again. You can probably find something useful in the bag of things I pulled. Why don't you come by after work and take a look?"

"You're assuming I can squeeze into your clothes."

"It's worth a try. I'm sure there's something here that will fit."

"Deal. I'll stop by on my way home from work. One more question before I let you go. I'm dying to know. What's Sally been up to?"

"She's been strangely quiet lately. I'm not sure why."

"I wouldn't look a gift horse in the mouth if I were you. She's caused more than enough trouble as it is."

"That's kind of how I look at it. Take care of yourself, Fran, and get busy on those interview questions."

After she hung up, Ellie began to wonder about Warren Blake. She'd never read any of his books. In fact, she didn't even know what kind he wrote. He just had sort of a household name. The only thing she could remember about him was that he'd been on several talk shows. Her attempts to picture the books that she'd seen displayed in the bookstore on the square didn't help. She could recall his name in big letters on the covers, but none of the titles came to her.

A quick internet search gave her the information she was looking for.

Warren Blake wrote ghost stories.

9

Ivy Garden had to look its very best for the famous guest scheduled to arrive on Monday. She gave Alice, Martha and Fred extra pay to work overtime cleaning, polishing and organizing. This was the hardest she'd made them work since Aunt Carolyn died. Fortunately, they didn't seem to mind. In fact, they were excited and willing to do whatever was needed to prepare for the author's arrival. They seemed to know more about Warren Blake than she did.

By Sunday evening, the weekend guests had wrung the last ounce of energy out of her. This group expected much more personal service than she was accustomed to providing. She passed out printed directions to places of interest, offered pamphlets, and gave out phone numbers for everything from battlefield guides to pretzel factory tours. Martha even made sack lunches for them. For a nominal charge, of course.

Ellie was almost asleep that night when her cell phone rang.

It was Wade. "I just wanted to give you an update. I'm getting closer to moving you and Sally through time."

"I'm really happy to hear this but I hope you don't mind if I hold my excitement until everything is ready." She had no idea how much longer that would be and neither did Wade. "Look, I have an important guest coming tomorrow and need to get some sleep."

"Really? Who?"

Everyone in town will be talking about it soon, Ellie thought, so he'll find out anyway. She may as well tell him. "Warren Blake."

"Warren Blake, the author? He writes the best ghost stories. I'll bet he can help me. What time does he arrive?"

"Hold on a minute. I'll not have you pestering my guests."

"I just want to ask him a few questions, that's all. Nothing to get worked up about."

"He's staying in town an entire week. You're bound to run into him sooner or later."

"Especially if I hang out at the inn."

"Come on, Wade. I've already asked you not to do that. Don't you have classes to teach at the college?"

"Afraid so but I already called in sick for this whole week to work on time travel. I really think I'm close this time."

"Do you know how many times you've told me you're really close and then there's another roadblock? Please don't get my hopes up until you've got this nailed. Okay?"

"Okay, Ellie. Just try to be patient. I want to this to work as much as you do."

Ellie was too tired to respond.

"One more thing," Wade said. "I'll make a deal with you about the author."

"No deals. Time to hang up."

"No, wait. I won't show up unannounced. You ask Mr. Blake when I can see him. Make an appointment or something. He should be able to find time for a college professor with an interest in his work."

"Good night," Ellie said and hung up.

Warren Blake looked nothing like the photo Ellie had found of him on the internet. Those head and shoulder shots never really present a true picture of a person. Taller than she'd imagined, this handsome middle-aged man filled her doorway with his broad shoulders. The sparkle in his bright blue eyes bore no resemblance to the stuffy egotistical person she expected.

"Hello," he said. "I'm Warren Blake." He extended his hand and gave hers a warm friendly shake and hung onto it a few seconds longer than necessary. "Thanks for making room for me here this week. Now that spring has arrived, the tourists are everywhere."

"My pleasure, Mr. Blake."

"Warren, please. And you are...?"

"Ellie. Ellie Michaels. Fred will give you a hand with your bags."

"It's okay. I can manage." After assembling his belongings in a neat pile near the door, he wandered through the parlor and dining room, admiring the antiques and asking questions about the house.

It didn't take Ellie long to forget that she was talking to a well-known author. He acted like a regular guy. The week-end guests who had checked out this morning had been more demanding than he was.

His information was already in her computer system since he'd registered online, so checking him in took no time at all. She ran through her usual orientation: breakfast serving times, front door key, room key, all part of a detailed speech that she could recite in her sleep. When she offered to walk him up to his room, he graciously accepted.

She'd set aside the Oak Room for him, thinking the large desk by the window would work out as well for him as it did for Harold, and she was right. Warren loved it. Her curiosity got the best of her then, and she had to ask, "So, what brings you here to Ivy Garden?"

"Some friends of mine stayed here recently and they raved about your place. I had to come and see it for myself."

He told Ellie about his friends, but she didn't recognize their names and couldn't remember anything about them.

Another lesson of innkeeping: Never underestimate the power of word of mouth advertising.

"Do you plan to do much writing while you're here?"

"Some. Research mostly. I'm starting a new book and still fitting the pieces together. It's a longer, slower process than most people realize."

"I can't imagine writing one book, let alone as many as you have. It would take me forever to finish the first chapter."

He smiled. "Enough about me. What did you do before you became an innkeeper?"

The inviting look in his eyes was engaging. Some people had a knack for getting others to talk about themselves, kind of like Fran, but this man was a master at it.

"Believe it or not, I was an Emergency Room nurse in New York."

"So, if sometime during the week I were to skin my knee, I'd be in good hands?"

"You'd be in good hands, no matter what," she replied, resisting the notion that he was trying to flirt with her. "Now I'll leave you to get settled. Please don't hesitate to ask if you need anything."

"I can assure you, I never hesitate." That gleam in his eye again.

Unsure exactly how to respond to that, she gave him her most professional smile and closed his door softly behind her. One thing was certain: this was shaping up to be an interesting week.

Ellie busied herself with the usual chores and a few hours later went into the dining room to set out the plates and glasses for the evening dessert. Apple cake tonight. She'd already sampled some. At this rate, she could skip dinner.

The house had been quiet the entire afternoon. Ellie had assumed all the guests were out, until she heard one of them coming down the stairs. It was Warren.

"You've been keeping a secret from me, Ellie."

She laid a handful of forks down on the sideboard. "Pardon me?"

"You didn't tell me that you're a reader. I found a book of mine on your shelf in the library upstairs."

He seemed so pleased to see it that she didn't want to admit all those books had been Aunt Carolyn's and she'd never picked up any of them herself. Too many years of textbooks and medical journals and not enough leisure time.

She managed to find what she hoped were the right words. "Our guests always enjoy a good book."

"So do I," he replied with a laugh. "Now, I was wondering if you might recommend a good restaurant for dinner."

Ellie went over to her desk, pulled out the list of dining suggestions that she maintained for her guests and handed him a copy. "There's a map on the back. Each one is marked. I also have a binder full of menus, if you'd care to look them over."

His eyes ran down the list way too fast for him to have read any of it. "Which one is your favorite?"

She named a few places for him. "It really depends on the type of food you like."

"Are you free this evening? I'd like to take you to dinner in appreciation for your hospitality."

Guests occasionally invited her to go out with them and her response was always a polite "No but thank you for inviting me". It prevented her from feeling obligated to anyone who bought her a meal and it kept the relationship with her guests on a professional level. There were a few exceptions, of course. Harold was one of them. Now it seemed Warren Blake was doing his best to become another.

"It's kind of you to offer, but…"

He wouldn't let her finish. "I know what you're going to say. You make it a policy not to go out with your guests, right?"

She nodded.

"Would you consider going if I told you that having dinner with me was part of my research?"

"Are you writing a book about New York City Emergency Room nurses who become innkeepers?" Two could play the teasing game.

Another easy laugh. "Hardly."

"What, then?"

"May I tell you about it over dinner?"

"How about over coffee and dessert in the dining room when you come back?"

"Quite the negotiator," he replied. "Okay. You win." After a short pause, he added, "This time."

She suspected that good-looking men like Warren Blake weren't accustomed to women who said no, but he'd made a valiant effort to hide his disappointment in her refusal.

"Enjoy your dinner." She tilted her head toward him in response to his theatrical bow and went back to her work. A few more tasks to finish and then she could sit down and relax for a while.

On her way from the laundry room to the cabinet in the dining room, a white cloth napkin fell from the stack in her hand and in her effort to catch it, she dropped them all. When she leaned down to pick them up, she noticed that the electricity in the air prevented them from lying flat. They seemed to float on top of each other.

"Grant?" she whispered. "Please tell me you're near." She hurried into the parlor and searched the surface of the mirror, waiting, listening, hoping. When Grant appeared, it was in a flash of light that made his face instantly visible in great detail.

His presence transformed her from Ellie into Ellen, a completely different person. It was like stepping out of a shell, from her world into his. The feeling of detachment from her everyday life grew stronger every time it happened. She protected her blossoming love for Grant from the outside world, acknowledging it only when he was near. The surge of energy around her was stronger every time he appeared also. Tonight, she could see his worried face in the mirror with astounding clarity as he spoke to her in a frantic voice.

Ellen. I am in desperate need of bandages for my men. We are running short of supplies. Your linens will suffice, if you will allow me to use them.

"Take them. Whatever you need. I'll just leave them there for you."

Thank you. Sally has locked hers away and I can spare no one to search for them.

"I understand."

You always do, Ellen.

His voice was calmer now, urgency turning to exasperation.

My men are dying all around me. I cannot stay a moment longer, but I promise to return to you as soon as I am able.

A promise. She could ask for nothing more. He lived among the chaos of men screaming and dying. If he turned his back on them to be with her, he wouldn't be the man she loved.

"I'll be waiting for you."

There is one more thing that I must tell you, Ellen.

"Of course. What is it?" Anything to keep him near her for a few minutes more. She needed him to hold her close again and bring to her lips the kiss that made her world dissolve into his. Hoping he would speak the words she longed to hear, she held her breath and waited.

The gentleman who arrived today. He mentioned a book to you.

So Grant was here earlier and she didn't know it. There was still so much to learn about him.

"Yes, I remember."

Read the book, Ellen. It is about me.

After Grant's swift departure, she forced herself to pull away from being Ellen, but it was becoming harder and harder to return to being Ellie. Staying Ellie wasn't as difficult once she was back. Transitioning was the tough part. Grant cared for her as Ellen and that's who she preferred to be whenever she could.

She checked her watch and kept an eye on the front doorway while exchanging pleasantries with her guests, expecting Warren to return at any moment. Every time she started up the steps to retrieve his book from the library, she was interrupted by a returning guest, a ringing phone, or a reminder of someone she needed to call to keep the third-floor renovation moving along. Her list of things to do never ended.

Then Warren walked in the front door, exuding his perpetual charm.

"How was your dinner?" she asked. "I hope you found a place to your liking."

The other guests' reaction to his entrance was fascinating. She hadn't mentioned to any of them that a famous author was visiting, and no one seemed to recognize him. They'd been busy milling around the dining room making small talk with each other when he came in. Yet one by one, they turned to take notice of him. Aunt Carolyn would have called it charisma.

"You mentioned the steakhouse earlier," he replied, "So I thought I'd give that a try."

"And?"

"Excellent food. Good service too. They even gave me a discount when I told them I was staying here all week."

"That's wonderful." Ellie needed to get busy building more relationships in town. Innkeepers should be telling their guests about discounts available to them, not the other way around. She made a mental note to ask Fran about how to run a joint ad with other businesses around town that included available discounts.

"I also ran into a friend of yours there."

Oh no. Did Fran jump the gun on her interview appointment? "You talked to Fran?"

"The newspaper reporter? No, I was talking about Professor Savage."

It was unusual for anyone to refer to Wade as "Professor Savage". He must have made quite an impression on Warren. She wondered if the encounter really was just casual. Wade was probably waiting to ambush the man as soon as he showed his face in town.

"Was Wade conducting research too?"

"Judging from the tone of your voice, I sense he's not a close friend."

Her relationship with Wade would be difficult for her to explain, especially since she didn't understand it herself. Ellie wasn't sure it was even a relationship. She knew him on a completely different level than anyone else. Better to let the subject of Wade Savage drop as soon as possible.

"You like the guy that much, huh?" he prodded when she didn't answer.

"Do you always get so personal with people you've just met?"

"Do you always answer a question with another question?"

The standoff ended in friendly laughter and they sat down at the dining room table with the last pieces of apple cake.

"Don't you even want to know what we talked about?"

"Why? Were you talking about me?"

"Here we go again," Warren said and they both laughed. "Wade is an interesting guy. His knowledge of Civil War history and local lore is quite extensive."

"True."

"The man has some unusual hobbies, though. Did you know he's working on some sort of time travel?"

"I've heard a few rumors," she said, trying to sound as matter of fact as she could under the circumstances. Better to keep the time travel topic at arm's length too. She didn't want Warren to get the wrong impression. "I do know that he's been fascinated with the original owner of this house for years."

"Ah, yes. I heard all about Sally."

"I'll bet you did."

He pushed his empty plate aside and then added cream to his coffee. "Do you believe in spirits, Ellie?"

Ellie searched Warren Blake's face trying to decide what to say. He'd been sparring with her from the time he set foot in Ivy Garden this afternoon. It was hard to tell if his question stemmed from general interest or resulted from the earlier conversation he'd had with Wade. Even though Wade was aware of her feelings for Grant, that's where it stopped. She and Wade had developed an unspoken understanding and exchanged no details. Ellie wouldn't permit Wade to intrude on her privacy where Grant was concerned, and she had no need to know what went on between him and Sally. She wasn't about to share her feelings for Grant with Warren Blake either.

A guest came downstairs with a dietary request for breakfast, rescuing Ellie from having to answer Warren's question before she was ready. It gave her a little more time to think.

After a brief apology for the interruption she said, "I think that acknowledgement of spirits is a very personal matter, similar to believing in God or the afterlife. We accept what we find plausible and what makes us comfortable and it's not the same for everyone. Some of it comes from the way we're raised and what we learn as we grow up. The pieces fit together differently for different people."

"A very benign statement coming from a woman who lives in a very haunted house."

"You didn't ask about the house. You asked me if I believe in spirits."

"So, what's the short answer?"

"Yes. I do believe in spirits."

"That's the answer Wade said you'd give me."

"Well, I've always been a fairly predictable person."

His eyes smiled at her over the rim of his china cup as he took another sip. He lowered the cup a little, swirled the remaining coffee around and studied it while Ellie waited for his next question.

"You really haven't read my book, have you?" he asked, raising his eyes and looking into her face.

She groaned. "I didn't realize it was obvious. No, I haven't read it, but I didn't tell you in so many words that I did, either."

"No, you just let me believe you did."

"To be honest, until you mentioned it this afternoon I wasn't even aware your book was upstairs in the library."

"Well, you do have quite a collection of books on those shelves. I can see how you might overlook one or two."

"Would it help to reassure you that I do intend to read it?"

He tilted his head just a little to the side as if evaluating her sincerity. "Maybe."

"How about giving me the condensed version over a second cup of coffee?"

"Only if it's decaf. I need my beauty sleep."

"Now who's being predictable?"

She felt him smiling at her back as she walked toward the kitchen to make a fresh pot of decaf, pleased that they'd reached this point in the conversation. Ever since Grant had told her the book was about him, she couldn't wait to get her hands on it and hoped when Warren returned, he'd share some of the details with her.

They carried their coffee into the parlor where she sat in her favorite chair and folded her legs underneath her. This way, she could face Warren and keep an eye on Sally's portrait at the same time. Just in case.

Sally had remained quiet for weeks now, ever since Grant conveyed her desire to live with Wade in the present. Maybe she was content to wait for him to bring her forward. Whatever the reason, Ellie was grateful. Grant's nocturnal activity was enough to keep her guests buzzing. Ivy Garden didn't need Sally to add anything more.

She focused her attention on what Warren was saying.

"Most of my books involve ordinary people living ordinary lives. Some are rich, and some are poor. They come from different walks of life in various time periods. In each book, the main character makes one small choice, the kind we all make every day, but it's a choice that ultimately alters the course of his or her life."

"I thought you wrote about ghosts. Isn't that why you asked me if I believed in them?"

"I asked you if you believe in spirits, Ellie."

"Aren't they the same thing?"

"Not exactly. A ghost is merely a disembodied spirit. It's the part you see, the part a spirit chooses to show you. Sometimes a ghost appears in the form that the spirit believes we will recognize."

"So, are there spirits in your book?"

"In most of them, but not in the one you have upstairs. There will be in the sequel though. That much I can tell you."

"Your new book sounds interesting already," she replied. "It makes me want to run upstairs and pull the earlier one off the shelf, so I can read it."

"I'll get it for you," he offered and was gone before she could protest. She'd only been making conversation and realized now that she'd better be careful about the casual remarks while Warren was around. The man took everything too literally. Were all writers like that? Harold had been the only one she'd known until now and he wasn't anything like Warren.

"Here it is," he announced, handing her the book.

Ellie gasped. A man in a Civil War uniform of Union blue stared at her from the front cover with sad brown eyes. Long chestnut hair turning gray at the temples hung in heavy waves that reached past the collar of his uniform. Scruffy brown whiskers covered most of his face, but Ellie knew in an instant that she was looking at a younger version of Grant Alexander.

She ran her palm across the surface of the front cover, then retraced the details with her fingertip. The only part of the picture that crackled with energy was the man's face. The same face she'd seen in the parlor mirror.

"What's the matter? Are you feeling all right?"

She laid the book down in her lap but couldn't take her eyes off the cover. "I'm fine."

"Your face turned white as soon as you saw the cover of that book, Ellie. There must be a reason for it."

"No, I'm fine. Really." She brushed him off and ignored the look of concern on his face. "So, what's the heart of the story?"

Warren looked into her face for a few moments. He must have realized she wasn't going to tell him anything, so he began the story. "In the mid-1800s, the young son of a wealthy Boston businessman finishes medical school and joins his uncle's practice. He refines his surgical techniques at a well-known hospital where he's recognized for his knowledge and skill. He is privileged, intelligent and handsome. Yet he's unhappy. Women fall all over him, but he's not attracted to any of them. Something is missing from his life and he doesn't know what it is. He decides to go out west to find it on the frontier."

A pioneer? This couldn't be the right story. Yet Grant's words to her were as clear now as when he spoke them. He had told her to read this book because it's about him. And there was no mistaking the face and the energy emanating from it on the cover.

"But then the Civil War breaks out," Warren continued, his enthusiasm for the story building. "And he feels it's his duty to enlist instead. As a Union Army physician, he follows the troops wherever they order him to go, treating, healing and comforting the wounded, the sick, and the dying."

"Does he ever discover what he's looking for?"

"I could tell you to read the book and find out, but that wouldn't be fair. Hopefully when you hear the rest, you'll want to read it anyway."

"No doubt."

"After the Battle at Chancellorsville, our hero is ordered to Washington, DC to help with the wounded coming in from the field hospitals. The conditions there seem insurmountable. So many to care for and not nearly enough hands to assist. When he's notified of a train pulling in with more wounded, he leaves the hospital to oversee the unloading and transfer of the new arrivals at the station. It must be done as quickly as possible, so the train cars can be loaded with badly needed artillery and supplies and leave again."

"The chaos in the railway station overwhelms him: the agony of dying men who were jarred and tossed about during the bumpy ride, the stench, the confusion, the cries for help. He's trying to do everything at once while accomplishing nothing. The recovered soldiers, ready to return to the front lines with the supplies, are waiting to board. Those who can never fight again but are stable enough to travel are being sent home to make room in the hospital. They fill every last available space in the train cars. At the center of all this, our hero's attention is absorbed by one mortally wounded soldier who wants to live long enough to see his home again."

Ah, thought Ellie, now it's beginning to sound like Grant.

"He gives the man a sip of water and suddenly the train starts to move. Our hero knows his orders are to stay in Washington, but he also knows the dying man won't live long if he doesn't stay with him. The train is moving faster and faster, each clack of the wheels on the track diminishing his chances of jumping off without injury. Within the next few seconds, he must make a choice: Stay on the train with the wounded man and keep him alive long enough to reach his home or jump off the train and let the man die. The doctor is a healer and his conscience won't allow him to let the man die, so he stays on the train. If it gets him into trouble for disobeying orders, he'll worry about it later. Then he learns the train is headed for Pennsylvania. It is June 29, 1863. He gets off the train at Hanover Junction, the old train depot down the road from Ivy Garden here, and takes the man to his home, one day before the Battle of Hanover and two days before the start of the Battle at Gettysburg."

Ellie let out a ragged sigh, unaware that she'd been holding her breath. "Is that the end?" she asked.

"Not quite." Warren stood up, put his hands in the pockets of his trousers, and walked toward the fireplace. He stared into the dying coals a moment, then turned toward Ellie. "Our hero remains in Hanover for the remainder of the war."

"So, he's here during the battle?"

"Indirectly, yes. He sets up a hospital in a farmhouse that's hit by artillery fire."

Ellie knew that wasn't really the end of the story. She also knew this entire conversation wasn't mere coincidence. "Warren, where did you come up with the idea for this book?"

"It came to me in a very vivid dream. Hard to describe. Like I was actually there as these events unfolded. I can still remember how exhausted I felt when I woke up, as if it happened this morning. I wasn't frightened by any of it, just wiped out."

Ellie understood that feeling quite well. "Was it the same with your other books?"

"No." He shook his head, the suave confidence and slick façade gone now. In a soft voice she could hardly hear, he said, "It only happened that way with this one, and it was my best book."

Ellie's mouth opened but nothing came out. She took the book from the table and held it. Thick silence hung in the air between them, broken only by the chiming of the clock.

Finally, she spoke. "You're telling me the truth, aren't you? None of this came from Wade."

"I swear to you Ellie, everything happened exactly as I described. As for Wade, he talked to me only about Sally, nothing else."

She nodded slowly. "This is the real reason you came here, isn't it?"

"Yes," he admitted. "It took me a long time to find this place, but I knew it was the one as soon as I walked in the door. I picked up the psychic energy in this room immediately, along with the tremendous emotion surrounding it." He closed the distance between them in three steps and touched her hand.

"Ellie, I came here to write the sequel," he said. "Will you help me?"

After Warren had gone upstairs, Ellie went about her normal end of the day tasks, not feeling very normal. On automatic pilot, she picked up dessert plates and coffee cups, loaded the dishwasher, and set up the dining room for breakfast. She carried the book back to her apartment, got undressed, and slid under the covers. Her eyes wouldn't stay open. Dropping the book on the nightstand, she gave in to her fatigue and turned out the light. As exhausted as she felt, sleep eluded her. In the middle of the night, she slipped her robe on and went out to the parlor.

"Grant?" she whispered. "Grant, please talk to me." She waited, listening for something. Anything. Silence and darkness were the only response.

Ellie turned on the light next to her favorite chair, intending to spend the remainder of the night reading Warren's book. Maybe she should start calling it Grant's book.

But when she went back to her apartment to get it, the book was gone. After making sure it hadn't slipped to the floor between the nightstand and the bed and checking under the bed, she retraced every one of her steps.

There was only one place the book could be, and it wasn't there. She returned to the parlor and sat in her chair, wondering if she might wake anyone by going upstairs to the library in case it was back on the shelf for some reason she couldn't explain. Then she looked up at Sally's portrait. She examined the woman seated in a chair as she had countless times before. Her eyes moved from the arrogant expression on Sally's face down to her dress and saw that Sally's hands were no longer resting in her lap. They held the book Ellie was looking for.

10

llie stumbled back to her apartment and crawled into bed. Once she recovered from the shock of what she'd seen, anger took over. How dare Sally take that book! She stormed into the parlor and demanded that Sally return it immediately. She had no right to take it and Ellie wanted it back. But the book was no longer in Sally's hands.

"What have you done with it?" She tried to keep her voice low enough to avoid waking anyone but loud enough to make sure Sally knew she meant business. She brushed away thoughts of a guest watching her shout at a picture on the wall.

Then she noticed the frame of Sally's portrait appeared a bit crooked. It didn't look that way a short time ago. She touched the frame to straighten it and the book fell to the floor. Ellie snatched it up and went back to her apartment, pleased with herself that she didn't let Sally get the best of her.

By the time Martha arrived in the morning to cook breakfast, she'd read half the book and loved every word. Warren's skillful writing ability made everything she read about Grant's early life come alive for her. It didn't matter whether everything she read was fact or a fictionalized account of Grant's life. She loved him more than ever.

When the early risers began to drift downstairs, Ellie had to set the book aside. Not wanting to take a chance on losing track of it again, she took it to her apartment and put it inside the drawer of her nightstand. Drawers probably don't keep tenacious spirits at bay, but it couldn't hurt.

Warren arrived in the dining room late and sat down with only a cursory nod to his fellow guests who had almost finished eating.

Ellie poured him a cup of coffee and noticed that the circles under his eyes were darker than hers. "Do any writing last night?"

"A great deal. Do any reading last night?"

"Once I found the book, yes."

He looked at her strangely. She'd been holding it in her hands when he went upstairs for the night.

"We'll talk later," she said and continued around the table making sure no one needed anything else before she started clearing the dishes.

When she and Warren were alone, Ellie reminded him about the interview. "Fran is planning to come by at two this afternoon. If you have time after that, I'll explain what happened with the book last night."

"Tell me again. Who is Fran?" he asked.

"The reporter from the town newspaper. You agreed to an interview when we talked on the phone before you came."

"Forgot all about it," he muttered into his pancakes.

"Will this afternoon still work out for you or do you want to reschedule?" When he didn't answer, she added, "Maybe tomorrow would be better?"

He looked up at her. "Maybe, but not today. Can I let you know in the morning?"

"Sure." She sat down in the empty chair next to him.

He stopped eating long enough to apologize for his brusque demeanor this morning. "It's just that the new book is off to a wonderful start and I want don't want to lose any momentum by breaking away for an interview right now. I'm still going to need your help. You haven't changed your mind about that, have you?"

"Certainly not," Ellie replied, relieved that he wasn't upset about something to do with the inn or the other guests. The purpose of his visit was to work on the new book and that's exactly what he was doing.

"Ellie, do any of your guests mention hearing noises during the night?"

She suppressed a slight smile, sure of what was coming next. "Why do you ask?"

"I should have known you'd answer with another question."

"Bad habit," she acknowledged.

He was smiling now, calmer and more relaxed than when he'd first come downstairs. He'd probably preferred to keep working but had torn himself away long enough to eat something. Now that he was here, the need to rush back to work didn't seem quite so urgent.

His description was the same as many others she'd heard directly from guests as well as through Alice and Martha. Footsteps, men's voices, occasional moans and cries.

"Could it be that I heard the voice of Dr. Grant Alexander?"

"Warren, I have no doubt about that, believe me."

"Do you tell your guests that?"

"I generally prefer to let my guests draw their own conclusions. I don't know most of them well enough to understand what they believe or don't believe about the spirit world. Rather than frighten them, I usually explain that this is a very old house with a lot of creaks and drafts that could cause some of what they thought they heard."

"A very neutral response."

"Maybe it's because I haven't decided if I like the idea of Ivy Garden having a reputation for being haunted."

He looked at her closely and lowered his voice. "But we both know it is, don't we?"

Fran was disappointed to hear she wouldn't be meeting the famous Warren Blake today but agreed to reschedule the interview for later in the week. Ellie promised to call as soon as Warren confirmed his availability.

As hard as Fran tried to talk her into getting together today, Ellie declined. She didn't want her own first impressions of the author to somehow influence the interview. Fran should print what Warren told her, not what she'd heard from Ellie.

Another reason she didn't want to meet Fran was that Warren's book was waiting for her and she wanted to finish reading it as soon as she could. It took every effort not to sneak a look at the last few pages, so she'd know how it ended.

At her desk, she opened her spreadsheet that detailed all the costs of the third-floor renovation, along with lists of completed items and those that still needed to be done. She made arrangements to have the parlor wallpapered at the same time as the suite. She'd been putting these projects off way too long. Then she slipped into daydreams about Grant's life before she knew him.

Ellie glanced out the front window and saw Fran strolling up the front walk. Amazing how quiet that car of hers had become after she got a new muffler. Fran had pulled into the driveway and Ellie didn't even know it.

She gave her friend a hug. "How are you, Fran? You look great."

"Wish I could say the same about you. How long have you been carrying those bags around under your eyes?"

"I'm just tired, that's all. Working too hard probably."

"Well get some rest. You look done in." With her back to Sally's portrait, Fran glanced around the parlor and into the dining room in search of the famous guest. "He didn't change his mind about the interview again, did he?"

Ellie shook her head. "No. Not that I know of, anyway. Where would you like to talk with him? The garden? The porch? Here in the dining room?"

"Any place where I can't see that woman's picture."

"Somehow I knew you'd say something like that," Ellie said and forced a laugh that came out sounding uneasy.

"Anything going on with Sally I should know about?"

"No. I think Wade's been keeping her occupied."

"Doing what?"

"Did you come to interview me or Warren Blake?"

"Curiosity always gets the best of me. You know that."

Ellie took her friend's arm and walked her out to the garden. "I had Alice wash off the patio furniture after breakfast this morning when I was convinced the sun was out to stay. Would you like to sit out here?"

"This is perfect. It's so beautiful back here behind the inn. I usually just breeze in and out the front door when I come here. I've forgotten how much land you have."

"Ivy Garden's spring flowers are just getting started, but the summer blooms and autumn color will be just as beautiful in their own way. Winter too, as a matter of fact."

"Admit it. You're just in love with the place."

"Truer words were never spoken."

Fran opened her mouth to say something and Ellie knew she was going to ask the meaning behind that cryptic response. Warren rescued her from having to answer.

"Good afternoon, ladies!" He waved to them from across the yard and swaggered toward them, more striking in his appearance than ever. Since the day he arrived, Ellie couldn't help but notice how handsome he was every time she saw him. Any woman would. But she felt no attraction to him whatsoever. He was a guest like all the others. A little more well-known than most, but still just a guest.

Fran's wide-eyed reaction was another matter. Her jaw dropped when Warren appeared, and Ellie had to poke an elbow into Fran's ribs to get her to close it again. She had expected this to serve as an opportunity for Fran to sell more newspapers and maybe market the interview to a few magazines. Instead, Fran was gushing over Warren like a schoolgirl. Ellie had never seen anything like this and it was downright comical.

Ellie left them alone for a few minutes and returned carrying a tray with iced tea and a plate of Martha's ginger cookies. She quickly excused herself, still marveling at change in Fran. It could be that she acted this way in all her interviews, but Ellie doubted it as she observed them from the kitchen window. No, Fran was instantly smitten by this man and having a hard time hiding it.

Then she saw Myra and George coming across the yard, big smiles on their faces. Ellie dashed outside to head them off. If they were coming to scold her again about Wade, they wouldn't be smiling. They must have recognized Warren.

"Hello, Ellie dear!" Myra called.

Fran and Warren tore themselves away from their absorption in each other just long enough for a nod and a smile and went back to their intense conversation.

"Hi Myra. Hi George," Ellie said. "How about coming inside for a glass of iced tea?"

"Oh, we thought we'd just join your friends out here." She leaned close to Ellie and said, "That's Warren Blake the author there, isn't it?"

"Yes, but he's very busy right now." She took Myra's elbow and guided her toward the back door.

"But…"

"I've been wanting to ask you to take a look at my schefflera plant. It's not doing so well, and you have such a wonderful green thumb. Would you mind?"

The expression on Myra's face told Ellie the flattery approach worked.

"Oh, well, of course. Glad to help. We can talk to Mr. Blake another time when he's not so busy." She turned to get consensus over her shoulder. "Can't we, George?"

"Sure." He followed the two women inside and they launched into a lively discussion about plant food, fertilizers, sunlight, and potting soil.

When the Kellers were ready to leave, instead of moving toward the door, they tiptoed over and stood in front of Sally's portrait as if to say goodbye to her. They studied her face for a few minutes, then looked at each other with a slight nod. It was the strangest thing.

"Ellie," George said. "I'm very glad to see that you're taking good care of Sally's portrait. It would be a mistake to do anything that might, well, bother her. Understand my meaning?"

"I think so, George. You don't have to worry."

Then it was Myra's turn to jump in. "I've noticed the light on quite often in that big room up on the third floor. A lot of workmen have been coming and going too. You weren't fixing up that room to rent it out, were you?"

"Yes, as a matter of fact, the renovation has been underway for a while now. I'm turning the big room into a guest suite. Why?"

"Well, that was Sally's room," Myra said as if that explained everything. "After her husband died, you know, she had to rent out the rest of her house to make a living."

"I know."

"No one's ever stayed there."

"I know."

"She might not like it."

"I guess we'll find out soon enough then, won't we?"

Myra and George exchanged glances.

"Everything's fine," Ellie assured them. Even if it wasn't, she wouldn't let George and Myra know it.

"I'm not so sure it's a good idea for you to keep letting that Wade Savage come around here," George told her. "You can't tell what he might be up to. If you want, I'll tell him myself that he better leave you alone."

"That won't be necessary, George." She hoped the firm tone in her voice got her message across. "Wade is harmless."

George didn't appear convinced, but he didn't argue with her.

"Well, we'd better be going," Myra said. "I need to get supper started before the news comes on."

Ellie almost had them out the front door, when Myra piped up again. "We can come back later to see Mr. Blake. How long is he staying anyway? Did he come here on vacation or something?"

"I'll let you in on a little secret," Ellie said in a loud whisper, watching Myra's face light up in anticipation of juicy gossip. "He came here to start a new book. Except for the interview he agreed to do for the newspaper, he's asked not be disturbed so he can work."

She looked them both square in the eye. "So, all of us will have to respect his wishes and give him the privacy he came here for. If not, he won't be back and we don't want that to happen, do we?"

George and Myra moved their eyes from Ellie's face to each other and back again, almost simultaneously. They clearly didn't like it but couldn't come up with a good argument.

Ellie had just ushered the Kellers out the front door, when Fran and Warren came in the back from the garden, discussing their plans for the remainder of the day.

"I decided to take Fran up on her generous offer to give me a historical tour of the Hanover area and on toward Gettysburg."

Fran just smiled. In fact, she blushed. Her smile widened even further when he turned to her and asked about dinner.

"We'll probably stop and have dinner at one of the old taverns somewhere along the way, Warren said. "If that's all right with you, Fran. Are you sure you have time?"

Boy, does she, thought Ellie, as her friend nodded with enthusiasm.

Fran gave Ellie a quick hug. "We'll just have to catch up another day. Sorry."

As the week went on, Warren and Fran spent more and more time together. Fran was having trouble keeping up at work with all the time she spent with Warren. When he told her he was coming back to stay at the inn at least another week, she requested the few remaining days of vacation time she had from the newspaper to be with him when he returned.

Ellie was beginning to wonder how Warren found any time to work on his book. Her question was answered at the end of the week when Warren was checking out.

"It's been a wonderful stay but I'm afraid I have to leave. I've learned a lot about the area, thanks to you and Fran. Much of the information I've gathered will be very helpful as the new book comes together. I have business to take care of which will probably eat up the next ten days or so, but I wonder if you might have room for me after that."

"The inn will be closed for the next three weeks for renovations and completion of the third-floor suite, remember? You're the last guest to check out until we reopen."

"Oh, that's right. You told me. I just forgot." He thought for a moment, then said, "Ellie, I was really hoping to come back here to finish my sequel. There is no other place to write it. Would you consider allowing me to stay during your renovation?"

"Warren, I really hadn't planned on any guests here at all until the work is finished."

"I won't be any trouble. I can get my own breakfast in town and promise to keep out of the way. What do you say?"

"Well…all right, only if you promise to be invisible."

"As invisible as my main character, Ellie."

He gave Ellie his planned check in date but when she asked him what date he would be departing, he hesitated. "Could we leave it open, Ellie? I'd like to stay as long as it takes to finish the book."

"If the suite is finished before the book is, you can be the first guest to stay up there if you'd like to."

"In Sally's room? You bet I would."

"I'll reserve it for you. Safe travels, Warren. I'll look forward to your next visit." And so will Fran, she thought.

Ellie had finished Warren's book and started reading it all over again. It was unbelievable how he was able to capture so much about the man she loved without ever having met him. She hoped to devote more time to reading now and settled down on the sofa in her apartment.

Immersed in the story, she jumped when she heard loud screams coming from somewhere upstairs. The book fell from her hand. She took off running, sure that someone had been hurt.

The cries were coming from the third floor. Ellie only made it as far as the second-floor landing where Alice fell into her arms, pale and breathless.

"Ellie, oh my God, Ellie," was all she could say.

Holding the shaking woman against her, Ellie was able to calm her down enough to determine that she was unhurt but very frightened. She led the way down the stairs with Alice following close behind keeping a tight grip on Ellie's shoulder.

Inside Ellie's apartment, Alice sank onto the sofa, clinging to the throw pillow like a life preserver. She rocked back and forth, letting out a soft wail but not talking.

Ellie sat beside her, rubbing her back with the palm of her hand in circular motions until the wailing subsided. Leaving her side only long enough to bring a glass of water and a cool wet washcloth, she continued to talk to Alice in a soft soothing voice until the woman relaxed and quieted down completely.

"What happened up there, Alice?"

"Remember when we had that talk a while back, about the noises and the moaning the guests would talk about? How they said the inn was haunted?" She wiped her face then laid the washcloth out straight in her lap and rotated it as she spoke, moving her fingers from one corner to the next. Compared to the way she'd been rocking earlier, this repetitive motion was an improvement.

"Yes."

"And that feeling like you're being watched, only nobody's there?"

"That too, yes."

"Well, that feeling's been strong up there in the new room. I mean, real strong. Some days when we were so busy in that room cleaning up after the workmen, I'd come down to get supplies and just feel her eyes on me when I pass by the parlor.

"You mean Sally's eyes?"

Alice nodded. "Those eyes would be looking straight at me from the picture when I'd get to the bottom of the steps and follow me when I walked to the center of the room. Glaring at me. Made my skin crawl, I'll tell you."

She stopped turning the washcloth long enough to wipe her face with it again and sip some water.

Ellie wanted to prod her into talking more about what had just happened, but her experience from working in the Emergency Room told her Alice would get to that sooner if she remained patient and let her tell the story her way.

"So today I wanted to clean the glass in the French doors that open to the widow's walk up there, you know? When those workmen started bringing in their tools and supplies this morning, they had to leave smudges on everything whether they need to touch it or not. I had to clean off all their finger-prints. I don't want anybody looking at those windows from the road and seeing that they're dirty. They'll wonder what kind of a housekeeper I am."

Now she was sounding like herself again.

"So I was drying the outside of the windows with my rag and Ellie, I'm telling you the absolute truth now, I felt myself moving closer and closer to that black railing up there. I felt like I was going to go over the top of the railing and all the way down to the front walk below and I couldn't stop myself. There was nobody up there in the room but yet something or someone kept pushing me. Like the strongest wind I was ever up against." Her voice cracked, and she tried to hold her tears back. "It scared me to death."

Ellie took her hand. "You're safe now. It's all over."

"It just kept coming, moving me one step at a time, back toward the railing. If it hadn't stopped, I'd have gone right over the railing and down to the ground." She shook her head. "That would have been the end of me."

"Was it your scream that made it stop?"

"I think so."

"Alice, I'm so sorry this happened. I ran upstairs as soon as I heard you call out."

She turned to face Ellie on the sofa, sitting close enough for their knees to touch. "I truly believe it was Sally." She said it slowly, pronouncing each word with deliberate precision.

"You think the spirit of Sally Brendel was trying to hurt you?"

"I'm sure it was Sally. She still lives here. I know that now. Don't you?"

Ellie took in a deep breath and let it out slowly. She had to be careful not to frighten Alice any more than she already was, while still giving her an honest answer.

"Alice, I agree with you that Sally still lives here. I've noticed how she manipulates what I see and plays tricks on me by moving things around. But this is the first time she's tried to hurt anyone."

"Maybe it's happened before but you never heard about it."

"What makes you think so?"

"Did you ever talk to the people who owned the place before your aunt bought it? Or the people before them?"

Ellie shook her head slowly. "I did some research last year after my aunt died so suddenly to see if they could offer any helpful information, but I was never able to track down the former owners." It could be that George and Myra Keller knew more about the experiences the previous owners had than they had told her about. It would help explain the strange way they behaved in the parlor the day they were chasing after Warren.

"I'm just saying maybe there's more goes on here than we know," Alice said.

Ellie reached over and patted her hand. "Why don't you get your things together and go home now? Get some rest and take tomorrow off. With pay. When you come back…"

"I'm sorry, Ellie. I made up my mind. I'm not coming back."

"Oh no. Don't leave because of what happened today."

"I don't want to, believe me. But giving Sally another chance doesn't sound too good to me either. She might succeed next time."

"Would you at least think about it tomorrow, and call me? I really hate to lose you, Alice."

"All right. If you don't mind my saying so, you'd better think long and hard about keeping this place. Suppose that happened to one of your guests?"

Ellie dialed the phone and listened to six rings before Wade answered.

"Wade, it's Ellie."

"What's up?"

"It's Sally. She tried to hurt my housekeeper."

"Alice? Is she all right?"

"Badly shaken up but at least she wasn't injured. It frightened her enough to make her quit."

"What happened?"

"Sally tried to push her over the widow's walk rail outside the third-floor suite. She was cleaning the windows in the French doors and says she felt herself being pushed to the rail."

"Sally's never done anything like that before. Maybe you shouldn't be so quick to blame her. After all, Alice is getting kind of old, isn't she? I mean, maybe she just got dizzy or something."

"I'm telling you it was Sally. Are you going to help me or not?"

"Okay. I'll be right over."

As soon as he walked in, Ellie insisted he go up to the third floor with her. She described exactly what happened and told him to do whatever it would take to make sure Sally never pulled anything like this again.

He still didn't seem convinced it was Sally's fault. "If what happened with Alice was really Sally's doing, it probably means she either doesn't like what you're doing with the third floor or she's getting impatient with my inept time travel efforts. I'm really close now, Ellie. Now that you're closed for renovations, I plan to spend a lot of time in your parlor to finalize the transfer. I need to be close to both the mirror and the portrait. And don't say you don't want me disturbing your guests, because you won't have any."

Ellie left him alone in the parlor and went back to her apartment. She breezed through the sitting area but slowed to take a second look at the small painting of the inn that Wade had given her. Something was different. Then she realized what it was.

In the painting, the shadowy figure of Sally Brendel now stood on the widow's walk with her arms folded in front of her. Smiling.

11

The house was quiet that night. No guests, no footsteps, no cries of wounded men. Ellie was alone in the inn. She rolled from one side of her bed to the other and back again in search of the comfort that would bring relaxation and sleep. But it eluded her.

Staring at the ceiling, Ellie fretted about the incident in the suite today and worried about having to find another house-keeper. Alice's shoes could not be filled easily. The woman was dependable, meticulous and worked as if Ivy Garden were her own home. She had become part of the inn and if she left, it would be another tie to Aunt Carolyn broken.

The picture on the cover of Warren's book stared at her from the nightstand. She'd finished it twice and hungered for the sequel. Before Warren left, she almost asked him for permission to read the pages he'd written so far. Common sense and good manners won out at the last minute, saving her the embarrassment of sounding like a member of his fan club.

Instead, she would spend some time working through details of the sequel with him when he came back. During the time he'd stayed here, they were up past midnight talking every night after he dropped Fran off. Ellie told Warren everything, starting with her first glimpse of the mist in the mirror.

Still wide awake, Ellie was unable to think of anything except Dr. Grant Alexander. Reaching for Warren's book on the nightstand, Ellie ran her fingers over the Grant's picture on the cover and spoke to him in soft whispers as only Ellen could. Then she got up, went to the closet, and slid Ellie's few remaining clothes to the side. Grant's medical box had been moved again. Sometimes she found it neatly stowed in the corner against the wall. Other times she found it on top of her shoes with the lid open and contents strewn about.

She pulled her 19th century dress from the end of the rack. Yes. She would put it on and hope that Grant would know what it meant. Now able to admit it to herself, she wanted far more than conversation. She wanted Grant. All of him. Tonight. Her desire for him consumed her thoughts.

Nothing would convince her that having him beside her on the bed had been a dream. He was truly there with her and she wanted him to return. Her dress, her hair, the lilac scent, everything down to the serene expression on her face helped her become the woman Grant sought throughout his adult life and never found, according to the story Warren wrote. She would be the center of his story's sequel. Starting tonight.

Ellen stood waiting for him in the middle of the parlor and whispered his name. When no sign of him appeared in the mirror, she closed her eyes and held her hands out in front of her, every fiber of her being alerted to any sign of his presence. Oh please, she thought. Don't disappoint me. Not tonight.

She felt a tingling burst of electrifying energy at her shoulder, just before he spoke.

Ellen. His gentle hand touched her arm.

"Yes, Grant. I've been waiting for you, hoping you would come to me."

How lovely you look. So radiant.

"I want to tell you…"

But he didn't let her finish. *I know.* He pressed his fingers to her lips. *I love you too.*

He understood her so well. Like no other man she'd ever known. Not only could he read her thoughts, he could read her heart.

Ellen closed her eyes and opened her arms to the mist that surrounded her in a rush of soft wind. When she felt him bend his head toward her, she lifted her face to meet his kiss. A long lingering kiss that shot sparks through her entire body.

His arm tightened around her waist as she felt herself being lifted from the floor. With his other arm beneath her knees, Grant carried her from the parlor and into her apartment where he set her gently on her feet next to the bed.

Over his shoulder, she saw that the door had been closed and locked. They were alone together now, and she wanted this night to last forever. She closed her eyes again, needing no more verification that his form was human, not merely the mist of spirit. For her, for tonight, he was a man. Her man.

Ellen, my dear. Would you allow me to unfasten your hair?

She felt his hands on her head and turned around, so he could reach the pins that held her hair in place at the back. One by one the hairpins came out and dropped to the nightstand. His hands stroked the long curls as they escaped, and she could hear his soft murmur of pleasure as he crushed them in his fist and then let them go.

She tipped her head back as he ran his hands through her hair from her scalp to the ends in long slow movements. Then her hairbrush was in his hand and he pulled it through her hair in easy strokes, arranging it on her shoulders.

Each slow deliberate stroke felt more exciting, more sensual than the last. She wanted to turn around and kiss him, but his gentle hand on her shoulder kept her back to him.

After he placed the hairbrush on the nightstand, she felt her earrings slide from her earlobes one at a time and she heard them drop into her jewelry box on the dresser. It was all she could do to stand still and wait for him to return to her.

His hands moved to her shoulders and then to her back as he wrapped his arms around her and drew her body closer. She could feel that the intensity of his excitement was as great as her own. There would be no turning back now. This was the moment she'd been longing for.

His fingers touched her neck just beneath her chin. He removed the cameo pin, held it a moment, and then placed it on her nightstand. When he began unfastening the hooks and eyes on bodice of her dress, she could hardly breathe. As he released the last one, the bodice slid from her shoulders and fell to the floor.

This time, the murmur of pleasure that she heard was her own, drawn out in a low moan from deep in her throat. His fingers traced the length of her bare arms and when they reached her hands, he brought them to his mouth and brushed his lips across the tips of her fingers.

She opened her hands to touch his face and stroked the long hairs of his beard. The curls at the back of his neck circled her fingers, welcoming her. The only way she could learn the details of his body was to touch every inch and memorize it, starting at the top. The pleasure he seemed to find in this heightened her own and he moved ever so slightly with her fingers, patiently, as if he understood how much she needed to do this.

The only thought in her mind kept repeating itself. *I love you. Oh, how I love you.* But she knew that words were no longer necessary between them now. His tender touch and the sense of having him near were all she needed. The thrill of Grant's single kiss at the base of her throat brought her entire body alive as never before.

Moving faster now, he helped her out of her long skirt and petticoat. She kicked them aside with one foot. Unable to feel him next to her now, she leaned forward to turn down the bedspread and sheet on the bed. With quick fingers, she removed her chemise and drawers and waited for him under the covers.

Sounds from across the room told her Grant was placing his uniform on the small chair in the corner, no doubt folding each piece into a neat pile. Soon he was there beside her. So many things she wanted to say but she dared not break the spell by speaking to him.

Desire overwhelmed them both. Long intimate kisses amid a tangle of arms and legs as they moved between and about one another brought them to a higher level with each electrifying stroke.

By the time she reached out to welcome him inside her, she'd lost all sense of everything else around her except this man. The rest of her world was gone and there was only Grant, filling her, consuming her and surrounding her all at once.

His short gasps of breath blended with hers in a chorus of delight that grew louder and faster. Fireworks exploded behind her eyes in flaming colors. Their dance of desire reached its crescendo with spasms of pleasure.

When their breathing slowed down and he moved to her side, she nestled into his shoulder. "I love you, Grant."

As I love you, my dearest, he whispered and ran his forefinger from her temple to her chin. She kissed its tip and he caressed her body one more time.

"Will you be here with me in the morning?" she asked, not wanting to hear the answer if it wasn't the right one.

I will always be here. It has always been because I was needed here, by my men. Now it will forever be because I love you so much and cannot bear to be away from you.

As she drifted off to sleep, her last conscious thought was a simple one. She never wanted to wake up.

But she did wake up. Quickly.

Heavy pounding on her apartment door brought her back to reality in a hurry.

"Ellie? Are you all right? Ellie!" Martha's voice carried a hint of panic.

"Yes. Just a minute."

She glanced at the clock on the nightstand and couldn't believe it was after 9 am. The alarm didn't go off. Then she realized it was because she hadn't set it.

"Ellie?" Martha again. Louder this time.

She groped around for her robe, but it wasn't in its usual place on the bedpost. Her nightgown wasn't in its usual place either. She was naked. In a heap on the floor near the bed lay her 19th century dress, and neatly folded on the chair across the room was Grant's uniform.

Ellie ran over to the chair, swept up the uniform jacket and held it to her face. Inhaling his scent, she stroked the heavy wool and closed her eyes but not for long. When she heard Martha's key in the lock of her door, she dropped the uniform and ran for the cover of the closet.

One more tap and the door swung open just as Ellie emerged from the closet in her robe. She rushed toward Martha, trying shield the clothing on the floor from her view.

"Sorry for intruding, Ellie, but you had me a bit worried. Are you all right?"

"Yes, just overslept, that's all. Give me a few minutes," she said, urging Martha out the door. "I'll be right out."

Ellie picked up Grant's uniform and held it to her cheek once again, longing for his return. Instead of hiding it, she would keep it on the chair right where he left it, where she could see it and touch it often. Anything to keep him close.

As much as she hated washing away the sticky sweetness that remained between her legs, she had to take a shower. By the time she drew the curtain back and emerged from the bathtub, Ellen was completely gone. She dried her hair, dressed, opened the door of her apartment and went out into Ellie's world.

Fred was pacing in the kitchen, carrying a stainless-steel coffee cup in one hand while rubbing his chin with the other. When he saw her, he set the cup on the table and hurried toward her.

"Ellie, they're coming today to put up the wallpaper in the parlor, you know, and well, we have a slight problem."

She pictured the pattern Wade had helped her select for the walls and the new rug she planned to add to the center of the room. The drapes she'd ordered had just arrived yesterday, but until Fred mentioned it, she'd completely forgotten the work was starting today. No more guests would be arriving until after the work was finished and everything was in its place again.

"What's the problem?" she asked.

"It's the parlor mirror, Ellie. We can't get it off. It just won't budge. None of my tools will work it loose and I sure don't want to do any real damage to it or to that wall, this being a historical place and all."

"Leave it alone! Don't touch that mirror." She glared at Fred as if he were a thief caught breaking into her house. Ellie couldn't allow anyone to move that mirror, not even an inch. Anyway, the handiest man in the world would never be able to budge it. She knew Grant wouldn't allow it to be moved. He was as protective of that mirror as she was because it was his doorway into her world. And as soon as Wade had everything ready, it would be her doorway into Grant's world.

"Don't touch that mirror," she repeated. "Don't let anyone touch it. Just leave it alone."

Fred stared at her with a stupid bewildered look on his face that infuriated her. She'd never lost her patience with the staff like this before but just couldn't help herself.

"You heard me. Don't move that mirror. Tell the decorators to just wallpaper around it."

Martha was staring at her now too. Neither of them said a word.

Then another thought struck Ellie. "What about Sally's portrait? Did you take it down?"

"Yes, but I just moved it into the back hall until they're done with the fireplace wall."

"Have them paper that wall first and then get the portrait right back up where it belongs immediately." Her voice sounded sharper than she intended but she saw no point in apologizing.

Ellie sipped coffee from the mug Martha handed her. "Thank you," she said in a quiet voice. She looked at Martha and Fred's faces. An apology was clearly in order.

"I'm sorry. I didn't mean to snap at you. Please forgive me." They nodded and scurried away, not wanting to trigger any additional sharp words.

The strong coffee helped clear her head but didn't bring her thoughts back to the business at hand. All she could think about was being with Grant. She glanced at her watch. Wade would be in class, assuming he'd gone to work today. He seemed to be working enough to earn a paycheck but took time away from the college every chance he could get. Even if he had gone to work today, she could leave a message for him to get in touch with her as soon as he got home. She refilled her coffee mug and took it to her apartment to call him.

The busy signal blaring from Wade's old house phone was a good indication that he had stayed home today. She picked up her purse and hurried out the back door. "I'll be back later.

Fred can manage the workmen while I'm gone," she called to Alice over her shoulder.

On her way across the yard to her car, she had brief second thoughts about the workmen who were coming. There was a time not long ago that she wouldn't have considered being away when anyone was coming to the inn to work on one of the rooms. With a little effort, she managed to ignore the tug of her conscience. Nothing mattered more than Grant.

Her hand was on the door handle of the car when she heard Warren Blake's voice call to her from the side porch.

"Ellie!" He put his book down on the chair and walked toward her. "Where are you off to in such a hurry?"

"Errands."

"I was looking for you this morning. I wanted to make sure you didn't change your mind about letting me stay during the refurbishing. Everything all right?"

"Fine. You can stay. No problem."

"I don't consider myself psychic, but I'm sensitive enough to know when something's amiss. What is it?"

Ellie looked down at the ground and let go of the door handle, but instead of facing him, she looked beyond his shoulder toward the barn. "Nothing's wrong, Warren. I'm sorry. I didn't mean to be rude."

"I'm not looking for an apology here. You just don't seem like yourself."

What an understatement that was.

"We both know I came here to work on my book, but I've hardly seen you lately."

"Things have been a little hectic around here."

"Evidently."

"Ellie, you won't even look at me. What's the trouble?"

"Nothing. Look, I'm on my way out right now and I'm not sure how long I'll be gone. How about if I come find you later?"

"I'm having dinner with Fran tonight. I promised to pick her up at seven."

No big surprise there, Ellie thought. "I should be back before then."

"I'll count on it. Be careful."

Ellie climbed into the car without another word and headed out the driveway. When she glanced into the rearview mirror, Warren was standing in the same spot, watching her drive away with a bewildered expression on his face. He'll probably go back to his book and forget all about wanting to talk to her.

After Fran told her about the fire last year, Ellie had driven past Wade's house out of curiosity. It wasn't far from Ivy Garden. His car was parked outside the house. Good. He must be here. She pulled up behind it, got out and hurried toward the front door.

"Wade!" She rang the bell, rapped on the door and rang the bell again.

He held the door for her with one hand while balancing an open book in the other. "Okay! Okay! Have a little patience, will you?"

"Sorry, Wade, but I have to talk to you."

The urgency in her voice got his attention. "You're ready to do it, aren't you?"

She nodded. "Yes, but…"

He grabbed her waist and started to spin around in circles, taking her with him. "I knew it! I just knew it!"

"Stop it," she said, pushing him away. "This is serious."

"Nobody knows that better than I do. I'm just glad you finally made up your mind to go through with it, instead of just talking about it." Then he started to laugh. "If you had changed your mind, the next thing on your list would be putting up the For Sale sign, because there'd be no way that Sally would let you stay after what you've doing to her room."

Ellie hadn't thought about it those terms, but Wade could be right. Well, she wasn't doing this for Sally's sake. Wade's either, for that matter.

"Will you get hold of yourself and listen to me?" She wished he'd settle down. He wasn't acting like someone she wanted to trust with her life but that's what she was about to do.

"Okay. Sure. Want a soda?"

"No. What I want is to sit down and have a serious conversation. Can you do that or not?"

The silly smile disappeared from his face. He went over to the dining room table and pushed a massive pile of papers and books over to one side. Then he brought a chair up to the cleared area of the table and went around to the opposite side and sat down.

Ellie sat down and folded her hands on the table and looked him square in the eye. "You said you could help me go back to 1863 through the antique mirror in the parlor and bring Sally forward through her portrait at the same time. I've been waiting for you to figure out how. You could keep fine tuning this forever and still not be satisfied that you've got it exactly right. I think you're close enough and I'm willing to take the risk that it will work. In other words, I came to tell you I'm ready to go."

"Okay, but…"

"We have to do it now, Wade." Ellie interrupted. She was trying hard to keep her emotions out of this. No need for Wade to know that making love with Grant last night is what drove her here today. She appealed to Wade's practical nature instead. "The mirror and the portrait are essential to this and I'm afraid something will happen to one of them with all the workmen around. It didn't hit me until this morning when Fred was trying to take the mirror off the wall, so the decorators could hang the new wallpaper."

Wade stood up suddenly and knocked his chair over in the process. "You didn't let them move it, did you? I need that mirror to stay right where it is."

"Don't worry. I told them to leave it alone and hang the wallpaper around it. The mirror was stuck so tight to the wall that nothing Fred tried would pry it loose."

"Did they move Sally's portrait? You should have told them to paper around that too."

"It's safe in the back hall. I told them to start with the fireplace wall and put the portrait back up as soon as they finished before doing the rest of the room."

"You mean they're working on it today? And you're not even there? Geez, Ellie!"

"I thought this was more important."

"Well, it is, but we can't let anything happen to that picture of Sally either. Why didn't you tell them to paper around Sally too?"

"Because it came off the wall with no problem. Wade, I truly believe Grant kept that mirror from being moved. He wouldn't allow the pathway to be disturbed in any way. It's his doorway into our world and my doorway into his. Wade, we've got to do this now before something else happens to get in the way."

"I'm really close, Ellie but this is precision work, you know? What if something goes wrong and you get stuck somewhere in between?"

"I don't care. I'm ready to go. Every time I'm with Grant, I have less and less desire to return to normal life. It's hard to describe. Almost like I'm someone else."

"That will help. It's exactly what you need to do. Become as much like Ellen as you can when it's time to go. I noticed you call him Grant now instead of Dr. Alexander."

Ellie nodded.

"What does he call you, if you don't mind my asking?"

"Ellen."

"It fits." Wade nodded. "I like it. Well, it sure seems like Ellen is becoming quite familiar with him. I mean, even a guy like me can pick up on these things, you know. I told you right off that day we had lunch that you were in love. It was written all over your face."

"I've never felt this way about anyone in my entire life. It's got to be the strangest courtship that ever was, except maybe for you and Sally, but when we're together…" Her voice drifted off.

"Are you saying he's done more than speak?" He leaned across the table and looked into her face. "Ellie, are you lovers?"

She looked down at her hands like an embarrassed schoolgirl and nodded.

"I was never able to get that far with Sally, but you've certainly given me hope. Gotta hand it to you, Ellie. Here I thought I'd have to spend the rest of my life putting together this puzzle of how to travel back to Sally, and you're making the whole thing happen for me because of your relationship with Grant."

"Let's not get carried away. I'm not back in 1863 yet and Sally isn't here yet either."

"Right. One thing at a time."

"By the way, your hair seems to have filled in a little. Actually, it looks much better."

"Tell Grant he's two for two on the cure rate scale."

"He'll be pleased, I'm sure."

As they continued to firm up their plans and refine the logistics, it occurred to Ellie that anyone listening to their conversation would be inclined to have them both brought in for psychiatric evaluation. They spoke in terms of other planes of existence in the same way other people talked about Maryland or Vermont. Maybe the strangest part was how weirdly conceivable it felt to her.

Outside the dining room window, low heavy clouds had moved in, bringing with them a rumble of thunder. Wade flipped the switch on the hanging lamp above the table. The light from above his head cast a dark shadow over his face, giving him a sinister look. Ellie tried to ignore it. This was no time to let in any creeping doubts about trusting Wade to pull this off.

"Okay, Ellie. The big question now is when are we going to give this time travel project of ours a go?"

"Wade, in my heart I'm ready now. My practical side tells me to take a little time to get things in order first."

"How long?"

"Let's plan on June 30. I need the rest of this month to take care of things at the inn and arrange my personal affairs."

"Okay. Good. I'll be ready by then. I'm sure of it."

"Oh my gosh!" Ellie said, staring in disbelief at her watch. "It's after six. I'm never away from the inn later than three. Never."

"First time for everything."

"Not this. I'll just have to pay Fred and Martha overtime for staying late." She picked up her purse and headed for the door.

"I'm amazed at you, Ellie. There was a time this never would have happened, because the inn was always the most important thing on your mind."

"The inn still is the most important thing on Ellie's mind," she said. "But you're talking to Ellen now."

12

arren Blake was waiting for her under the cover of the side porch when she returned to the inn and waved as she drove in. He'd changed from his jeans and polo shirt into a sport coat, dress shirt, and slacks. Another date with Fran, Ellie remembered.

The cool air from the coming storm helped to clear her head after the long afternoon with Wade. "Warren, I must apologize to you for my hasty departure earlier. Can we sit down for a few minutes?" She owed him an explanation but suddenly, she wasn't sure how much to tell him. At least he was patient and waited for her to gather her thoughts. Then, after a deep breath, she just blurted it out. "I'm going back to 1863 to be with Grant on June 30."

"What?" Warren's jaw dropped. "I know Wade has been talking about this for months but really, Ellie? Are you sure you want to go through with this? I mean, think of all the things that could go wrong."

"I want to be with Grant more than words can convey. He's all I think about. And if something goes wrong, well, I'll just deal with whatever happens." Somehow it was easier to talk about her feelings with Warren.

Once Ellie started talking, she couldn't stop. Her conversation with Wade and her plans to organize everything before she left all came out in a gush. She left out the scientific minutiae that Wade relished so much and kept to the concept of her pathway to the past through the mirror.

"Ellie, I may be out of line by asking this, but if you're really going to do this, would you allow me to be with you when you leave?"

She didn't hesitate. "Yes, Warren. If all goes well, it will certainly add to your book. Besides, there won't be any other guests around until after the refurbishing is done. You're welcome to stay as long as you wish."

"I'll plan on it." He put his hand on her arm and leaned toward her. "Ellie, I still can't believe you're actually going to try this. If there's anything I can do to help you, before or after you go, please tell me."

"Actually, there is one thing. I don't want you to mention any of this to Fran. You can tell her after I've gone. She'll probably feel hurt that I didn't say goodbye, but if I try to tell her before I go, I'm not sure she'd understand, and that will cause more hurt. I need you to help her with that, ok? You and Wade are to be the only ones who know, and I want to keep it that way."

"What will happen to Ivy Garden? Have you thought about that?"

"I've thought about a lot of things, Warren. I intend to spend the next week putting everything in order. Ever since Wade and I first started discussing it, I've been working through it in my subconscious mind without realizing I fully intended to go through with it. I hadn't even spoken of my intentions out loud until today." She squeezed his hand and went inside.

The next few weeks flew by in a flurry of activity. She put Fred completely in charge of the refurbishing, gave Alice few weeks of paid vacation. Then she invited Fran to come by and together they went through Ellie's closet, pulling out all the remaining clothes and accessories that she no longer wore. Fran was delighted that most of the clothes Ellie was giving away actually fit her.

Then Ellie spent time alone writing her last will and testament. The hardest part of all this was going through legal arrangements with the lawyer to ensure that there were no loose ends regarding Ivy Garden. Since she had no heirs, the lawyer agreed it was a good idea to have all her wishes in writing.

All the earlier guilt from Aunt Carolyn's death returned and added to the emotional and physical drain. She would never have enough time to give proper attention to everything, but she wouldn't even consider a delay. She had made her decision and had no desire to change it.

She was ready.

The night before her travel, Ellen sat in the disheveled parlor and faced the mirror. She smoothed her long skirt and petticoats, and breathed deeply, inhaling the aroma of lilac. With her fingers on the brooch Grant loved, she whispered his name. "Grant. I need to talk to you."

Nothing.

"Grant? Are you there? Please come to me."

She waited. Still nothing.

Oh no, she thought. When Warren had asked her about what might go wrong, it hadn't occurred to her that she might lose her connection to Grant before she even reached him. She closed her eyes, picturing his face, willing him to speak to her. A sudden chill moved through her body. She stood and walked up to the mirror. As if a switch had been flipped, the solitude of the house became instant chaos, screaming, banging, clattering, and every sound imaginable engulfed her.

Ellen. Please forgive me. I am surrounded by this terrible calamity. The suffering here is beyond words.

"Oh, Grant. Thank God. I was afraid you wouldn't come to me tonight of all nights."

I would be with you every night if I could, my dearest. I hope you know that.

"Soon you will be with me every night, my love."

Whatever do you mean, Ellen?

"I have found a way to join you in 1863. It involves far more than I can explain to you now. I just want you to know that tomorrow and forever after, we will be together."

Truly? I do not quite understand, but I hope with all my heart that it can be so.

"It will be so. I promise."

Until tomorrow, then. I await you.

Ellie wasn't nervous until Wade arrived.

"Sally's ready. She can't wait to get here and fix up my house the way hers used to be. She promised to let go of this one. Finally."

Good, thought Ellie. Another loose end tied up.

She checked and rechecked every detail of her appearance. Every item she wore was an authentic replica of 1863 clothing, down to her underwear. She pictured herself in this very parlor with Grant during the Battle of Hanover on June 30, 1863. It kept her mind occupied and cut down on the annoyances Wade kept creating. At last, he announced it was time.

Warren approached her and took both her hands in his. "Regardless of how things turn out, this night will be the climax of Grant's story. As it is, your story is so entwined with his, that you will be together forever between the covers of my last book."

"Your last book?" Ellie was surprised. "A great author like you could go on writing for years."

"There can be no better book than the one you've helped me write, Ellie. I'm not sure yet what I'll be moving on to, but it won't be another book."

Ellie had an inkling what might lie ahead for him but didn't say anything more.

She squeezed his hands, kissed his cheek and gave him a warm smile.

Ellen faced the mirror and followed Wade's instructions.

The speed was incredible. She felt herself spinning through one tunnel after the next at an unbelievable rate. She had no idea where she was, but the brilliant colors and bright lights that sped past her shone like nothing she'd ever seen before. At first their beauty fascinated her. But soon the colors blurred, and the intense light grew so bright she couldn't keep her eyes open. Squeezing her eyelids tight didn't keep the bright light from penetrating them. She covered them with her hands. Her head pounded.

She was whirling faster and faster. Dizzy and sick to her stomach, she fought the growing lump of heaviness inside her chest. Her mouth had never felt so dry, but she tried swallowing anyway and gagged.

The relentless rush of air was turning into a roar. Pain in her ears now. Sharp pain. Covering her ears with her hands didn't help. The pressure pierced the inside of her ears and filled her head.

Her hands moved all over her face and head, trying to keep out the light and the noise. The pain was becoming unbearable. Frightened, she tried to wake herself up to make it all stop. She was screaming now. Surely Wade had the ability to stop her from being propelled through this tunnel but her cries for help were lost in the void. When she thought she couldn't stand it a moment longer, everything went quiet and black. It was over.

She floated above the piano in what looked like the parlor of Ivy Garden, but it was a wreck. Blood everywhere. Men screaming, supplies strewn around on the floor, and men in blue uniforms rushing from here to there.

She made it! Ellie was thrilled to have survived it all. She had actually arrived here in the parlor in 1863. Where was Grant? She needed to find him but first she went to the mirror, hoping the incredible journey she'd just taken hadn't totally ruined her appearance. Fear gripped her heart when she realized that she wasn't able to walk across the floor. She looked down at her body, but it wasn't there. It felt like it was, but she couldn't see or touch any of it. The misty shapes that shifted around her were all that was left. No matter how much she wanted the familiar mist to be Grant, it wasn't him. Then it struck her. The travel through time was too much for her and the mist around her was now all that was left of her body.

Ellen Michaels was dead. The realization didn't frighten her. She felt surprisingly calm and peaceful. This wasn't anything like she expected, not that she'd really thought much in terms of her own death. She had fully expected to come through this as a living person and not arrive as a spirit. The strangest thing was not having a body any longer.

But if she had died, why wasn't Grant here to meet her? She sensed his presence before she saw him and rushed through the air toward him. But he didn't see her. He didn't even know she was there. Understandable on one hand, amidst the chaos, but he knew she was coming, didn't he?

Grant. It's me. Ellen.

He lifted his head and appeared to hear her but didn't speak. Taking a handkerchief from his back pocket, he wiped his forehead and slowly made his way toward the door to the courtyard at the back of the house. He crossed the courtyard and went around to the back of the barn.

She followed him through the mist and fog that swirled around her to where he stood alone, and she flew into his arms.

Grant. I'm here. Can you hear me? Can you see me?

"Ellen, my dear. Oh, Ellen. It is indeed you. I can feel you now through the mist and I can hear your voice, but I am unable to see you clearly. How thrilled I am to know that you are here but your physical body did not survive the transition, did it? Were you hurt? Do you feel any pain?"

It was a terrifying journey, but I am not hurt. I am just so very sorry that only my spirit is here with you. Just as you hovered near me in my own time, so I will always be near you in your time. Nothing can keep us apart.

"After you told me of this last night, I have thought of nothing else. Although I cannot understand how you were able to accomplish it, I hope you know my love for you has not changed."

Hold me closer. Please.

And so he did. For a very long time.

Warren Blake and Wade Savage sat together in the parlor, staring at the mirror in silence. Warren finally spoke. "I watched her fade into that mirror with my own eyes and I still can't believe it."

"Well, that's the way it was supposed to work, isn't it?" Wade replied. "No real glitches that I could see."

"If this is what she really wanted, then I just hope she's ok and that she'll be happy."

They both felt a distinct crackling of electricity in the air at the same time. Wade stood up and crept over to the mirror as if he might disturb something if he moved too fast but he could see nothing. Then his attention turned to the portrait.

The mist that had been Sally Brendel gradually took shape in front of her portrait. Then, the cloud faded and she stood before Wade.

"Sally Brendel." Wade said. "Welcome home."

Her demeanor evolved from a frightened woman in foreign territory to the lady of the house in a matter of minutes.

Turning toward the portrait above the fireplace, Sally shrieked, "My portrait! What have you done?"

Wade and Warren stared at the portrait in disbelief. In the portrait that had been Sally's was the face Ellen Michaels, appearing exactly as she did when they last saw her, wearing her lavender dress, the brooch she loved, and a sweet gentle smile.

After a while, Wade broke the silence. "Sally, the only way I could bring you to me was to send Ellie back to your time. I wanted you here with me. You know that, don't you?"

"Did you have to ruin my portrait?"

"I didn't know it was going to change like that. Besides, we don't need it to communicate anymore. We're together now and I'll make it up to you. Promise."

Turning to Warren, he said, "We better get this off the wall. I'm not ready to explain it to anyone." Together they carried it to the back hall next to the stairs while Sally sat at the piano, wailing with her head in her hands. Warren said a quick good night and went to his room, leaving them alone to sort things out.

Wade calmed Sally down, explaining that she would be happier at his house. He would take her there in the morning. It was much more modern than the inn and she wouldn't be surrounded by unhappy memories there. He was sure that was what she wanted.

Where's Dr. Alexander? Is he with her now?" Sally gestured toward Ellie's portrait.

"I don't know if Ellie is with him or not. It doesn't matter now. I want you to let go of the heartbreaks from your past, including the doctor. I know you loved him once, but it's time for you and me to be together." She softened at this and allowed Wade to take her hand. He led her upstairs to the suite where they spent the night.

Early the next morning as they were leaving, Sally paused near the grand piano in the parlor and ran her hand across the surface. "This is mine," she told him. "It belongs to me and I want to keep it."

"We'll come back for it," Wade promised. Anything to make her happy.

The next morning, Martha pounded on the apartment door. "Ellie, are you all right?" She had returned to the inn after her vacation and wanted to go over her shopping list with Ellie before heading to the market. It wasn't unusual for her boss to be away afternoons sometimes, but it was early, and no one was about. The bad feeling she had when she arrived at the inn just kept getting worse. She couldn't explain it. Something was just wrong, that's all. Why would Ellie have left her cell phone on the kitchen counter? She always took it with her.

Besides, it's just not like Ellie to be gone when she knew that Martha had things to discuss with her today. Twice she checked the bulletin board by the back door, hoping to find a note from Ellie but there was no note anywhere. She used her master key and let herself into the apartment.

"Ellie?" Martha wandered from the sitting room to the bedroom, then checked the bathroom, muttering to herself, clearly bewildered. "What could have happened to her?"

Then she noticed the Civil War officer's uniform jacket on the back of the bedroom chair and the pants folded on the seat cushion. "This doesn't make any sense. Better call somebody." Martha went through every room in the inn and found no clues about Ellie's whereabouts. Could Sally have pushed them all off the widow's walk so fast? She didn't think so. Martha went to the phone and called the police.

An hour later, a uniformed police officer accompanied by a man in flannel slacks and a sport coat arrived, introduced themselves and sat down. Each took a small notebook and pen from his pocket. They questioned the pale and shaky cook and wrote down everything she said, including the parts about spirits making noises during the night and one particularly evil spirit that tried to kill their housekeeper.

Although they asked several more questions, poor Martha didn't really know anything more and couldn't help. All she could say was that she came to work this morning and Ellie was gone. Her boss always slept in her apartment and was always there for breakfast. After assuring them that she would stay and take care of things as best she could until all this got sorted out, Martha insisted there was simply too much work here for one person. It was important that these men knew what she was up against. After all, the inn had kept the four of them busy before Alice quit and now with Ellie unaccounted for, Martha could only do so much by herself.

Even their handyman, Fred, was gone. After the incident with Sally up in the suite that drove Alice away, he had decided the time had come to move out to California where his daughter lived. He'd told Martha that his daughter had been after him to move in with her family, what with their big house and all. He didn't want to admit it, but Martha knew that the spirits in the house had spooked him too.

Before the police left, Martha announced that she was quite capable of using the inn computer system and if Ellie hadn't turned up by the noon, she would cancel the following week's reservations. No one would be staying in the suite, that's for sure.

Just as the police stood up, George and Myra appeared at the front door wearing frowns.

"What's happened, Martha dear? Is everything all right?" When she didn't answer, they turned their attention to the policemen.

George and Myra clearly expected a full explanation for the presence of law enforcement, but the men seemed reluctant to reveal much. It didn't surprise Martha. After all, those men didn't know George and Myra and probably wouldn't like them if they did. Martha sure didn't.

As soon as the Kellers heard the words "Ms. Michaels seems to have vanished", they wasted no time in pointing the police in the direction of Wade Savage. "We tried to warn her to stay away from him," they said. "Ellie didn't take us seriously enough and kept letting him come around. Now look what's happened."

Then they turned to Martha. "What happened to Sally's portrait?" Myra asked.

"I didn't notice it was gone until just now." With a slow shake of her head, she sank down onto the sofa, clearly bewildered. "Last time I saw it was when the workers hung it back up after they painted in here."

"Well, it's gone now," said George. "No wonder you've got trouble here."

The police ushered the Kellers out the door and assured Martha that they'd get to the bottom of all this. Before long, they arrived at Wade's house and inspected the smoldered remains of his barn. Wade admitted he had built and rebuilt his time machine and acknowledged that this was the cause of the first fire. He acted nervous and frightened but answered all their questions and didn't try to hide anything from them. When they asked him when he had last seen Ellen Michaels, he told them she had gone back to 1863. He insisted Ellie was all right but gave no satisfactory answer that would explain how he could be so sure.

The two men exchanged glances, put their notebooks away, and took him to the police station. After more questioning and much discussion among themselves, they agreed to allow him to go free, as long as he didn't leave town. They warned him to expect to return for additional questioning as the investigation continued.

Wade was still his own worst enemy. He tried to tell them not to waste their time because they wouldn't find her. She wasn't dead, he insisted, but had simply vaporized from this particular place in time.

After the men left, Sally came out from the kitchen. She had already started making plans to return Wade's farmhouse to the way it was when she knew it before the war. She liked his house better than the one she had lived in anyway and often admired it when she rode past it on her way into town all those years ago. It was true that the inn was filled with bad memories and she didn't want to stay there. All she wanted from it was her piano.

Later that morning, Martha had just returned to the inn with some cleaning supplies and nearly dropped the bags when she saw Warren Blake sitting in the dining room. He appeared preoccupied with his papers and hardly seemed to notice that Ellie was nowhere in sight. He was not supposed to be here anyway. All reservations had been cancelled. Martha was sure of it.

"What are you doing here, Mr. Blake?"

"Hello, Martha. Ellie agreed to let me stay a while longer because I was making such good progress on my book. By the time I came to a stopping point and came downstairs to see what all the commotion was about, everyone was gone."

"Have you seen Ellie?"

"Not this morning, no."

"She's nowhere to be found. That's why the police were here. It's just not like her to leave without saying anything."

"I'm sure she's all right."

"Well, I'm not. Give me a few minutes to put these things away, brew a pot of coffee and I'll make you some breakfast. Then you and I will comb every inch of this place and try to find out what happened."

Martha brought two omelets and some toast over to the table and sat down across from Warren. He looked like he had aged ten years since he first arrived.

Martha admitted that she sometimes heard footsteps on the stairs early in the morning when she came to work but convinced herself that it was just another one of those strange sounds she had become accustomed to during all her years working at the inn. "Now that I think about it, maybe it was somebody who came back, broke in and kidnapped Ellie or worse. I don't know what to think."

"Let's not jump to conclusions, Martha." Warren wasn't quite ready to bring up the subject of time travel with Martha and he sure didn't want to discuss the portrait with her right now. "Better to let things play out with the police investigation first. "It does seem strange not to see her bustling around here, taking care of things."

"I know. Maybe it would be best if I stay here at the inn until this gets resolved, one way or another. Somebody's going to have to keep things running around here what with Alice and Fred both gone and Ellie missing."

"That's a good idea, Martha. Why don't you move into that room next to the stairway across from my room until Ellie comes back or until her whereabouts can be confirmed?"

Martha nodded. "Okay. That way, I'll be here in case there's any news." She liked Mr. Blake and even though he didn't talk much, it gave her some comfort just knowing he was nearby.

Warren did as Martha asked and went through the entire inn with her, but they found no clues to Ellie's disappearance except for some strange clothes in her bedroom. In the middle of the desk in the corner of her apartment he spotted a document titled "Last Will and Testament" along with a letter. Warren slipped them into his pocket while Martha was in the next room.

He had postponed calling Fran for as long as he could. He didn't give her any details, just told her he needed her to come to the inn as soon as possible. Of course, she dropped what she was doing and came right over.

"What could have happened to her?" Fran kept asking him. "It's not like her to just disappear. This has to be foul play."

"The police have already been here and they're working on it, but we should be prepared in case it's not good news."

"What do you mean, Warren?"

He tried to tell Fran that he just felt in his heart that Ellie was gone for good, but she wouldn't hear of it and preferred to put her faith in the police department.

"They'll probably want to interview you and me too," Fran said. "Maybe there's something we saw or heard that was important, but we just didn't pay attention to it."

"I suppose that's possible, but I don't know what it would be."

"You don't think that crazy professor Wade Savage had anything to do with it, do you?"

"Let's just wait for the police to do their work and see what they come up with."

"There's something you're not telling me, isn't there?"

"Sit down, Fran."

They sat together on the sofa in the parlor. Warren put his arm around her and they sat quietly for a few minutes. Then he turned to her and took both her hands in his. "How much do you know about Dr. Grant Alexander?" he asked.

"I know that he supposedly took care of wounded soldiers here during the Civil War and that Ellie believed she could see him and talk to him. I've seen that box of instruments from the attic that belonged to him. What does the doctor have to do with Ellie's disappearance?

"She was very much in love with him. Wade Savage convinced her that he could send her back to 1863 to be with him. He was able to use that mirror on the wall over there as the portal. I was here last night when she left."

"Oh God. I can't believe it. Then we'll never see her again, will we?" Her face started to crumple, and Warren held her close, holding back his own tears as she sobbed.

As soon as he found the letter and the will in Ellie's room, he notified the police. The letter confirmed Wade's story and the police found no other clues. The search for Ellie Michaels was eventually called off.

Weeks later, Warren sat next to Fran in the estate attorney's office, occupying the same chair Ellie sat in as she prepared the will that the attorney was about to read to him. This was merely a formality since he knew what it contained. He had been looking forward to seeing the expression on Fran's face when she heard the news that the attorney was about to give her.

Warren and Fran were about to inherit the Ivy Garden Inn.

That evening, they dined at Hanover's finest restaurant in honor of their dear friend. It would be up to them to plan a memorial service for Ellie. The notice that Fran had prepared would be in the newspaper tomorrow. It said Ellie's death was accidental and details were sketchy. Warren filled their glasses with champagne and they raised them to toast their dear friend. "To Ellie," he said. "May she live forever in our hearts and in the heart of her beloved Dr. Alexander."

"We may never be as good at innkeeping as she was, but we'll give it our best shot," Fran added.

The entire town attended Ellie's memorial service. Everyone who knew her was taken in by her warm kindness and generosity. The service was simple and sweet. Just the way she would have wanted it.

Wade had made arrangements to move the piano to his place the day after the service. Sally came along to take one last walk through and pick up any items she felt were hers. Fran didn't care and said that Sally could have whatever she wanted just as long as she never came back to the inn. Warren, however, held Wade and Sally to their agreement to take only the piano.

Warren went downstairs to give Wade and his crew a hand. They were taking the piano out through the French doors leading to the side porch that were put in by the former owners. He almost bumped into Sally on the stairway.

She lifted her skirts above her ankles and turned to run when she saw him, but he reached out and grabbed her arm to stop her.

He relaxed his hold on her arm when she stopped pulling away.

"And who might you be, sir?" she asked.

"My name is Warren Blake. I'm a writer. I wrote the story of you and Dr. Alexander and this house."

"Ach! There ain't no story about me and the doctor, I can tell you that much."

"You still don't like him, do you? Even after all these years."

"Why should I? That man ruined my life, he did."

"Well, the doctor is gone now, and you're here instead."

"Look what they done to my house! It was fine just the way it was before the war."

"Then there's no need to go through the whole house again, is there?" he said, steering her back down toward the parlor. He wasn't about to let her loose in the house by herself.

After Wade and Sally left, Warren wandered around the inn, making mental notes about a spotlight he wanted to add above Ellie's portrait and ways to fill the corner where the piano had been.

When Fran pulled in the driveway, Warren was waiting for her. She ran from her car to his arms in nothing flat. She didn't even close her car door before going inside with him. He helped her unload the few items she wanted to bring to the inn. They put Fran's things down in the parlor and paused for a long lingering kiss. "Welcome home, Fran," Warren whispered. He took her hand and led her upstairs.

Ellie smiled at them from her portrait as they passed by.

EPILOGUE

Hanover, Pennsylvania
June 30, 1863

D r. Grant Alexander called out through the chaos to his assistant, as a deafening explosion shook the walls of the inn. He raised his eyes in time to see the room above his head crash through the ceiling, burying him in the rubble with the dead soldier still clutching his hand.

Dr. Alexander's death was instant and painless.

Waiting for him on the other side, was his beloved Ellen, reaching out through the mist to take his hand. Released from the physical bonds that kept them apart, their spirits swirled and soared together to the world beyond where they would live and love together for all time.

Made in the USA
Monee, IL
05 October 2020

44022675R00142